D0941675

THE SECRET AT
LONE TREE COTTAGE

Books by

CAROLYN KEENE

Nancy Drew Mystery Stories

Dana Girls Mystery Stories

Leslie Mann

THE SECRET
AT
LONE TREE
COTTAGE

By

CAROLYN KEENE

Grosset & Dunlap, *Publishers*
NEW YORK

CONTENTS

The oncoming craft bore down swiftly upon the
defenceless little launch

The Secret at Lone Tree Cottage

CHAPTER I

Miss Tisdale Disappears

"Ooh—hoo! *Jean!* Hurry!"

"Ready in a minute, Louise."

Louise Dana waited at the head of the stairway. She was a pretty, dark-haired girl of seventeen, one of the most popular sophomores at Starhurst, a boarding school for girls at Penfield.

"Miss Tisdale asked us to meet her at four-thirty, and we're ten minutes late already," she called.

A moment later Jean came scurrying out of their study into the hall, cramming a hat down over her blonde, boyish-cut hair. She was a year younger than her sister, gay and impetuous, with laughter in her blue eyes and a humorous tilt to her nose.

As they reached the lower hall and ran toward the front entrance, they saw a tall girl

1

with a sullen face emerge from the office of the headmistress.

"Hello, Lettie Briggs! Don't you wish you were coming with us?" asked Louise.

"I wouldn't be a teacher's pet for anything," said the girl loftily.

"She's jealous because she was not invited!" whispered Jean as the two girls sped down the front steps.

Miss Amy Tisdale was waiting at the wheel of her smart little coupé in the driveway. She was a pleasant-looking young woman in her late twenties, and though quiet and reserved, was so gracious and sympathetic that no teacher was better loved by the girls. Moreover, the splendid work done by the students in her English classes was evidence of her ability to inspire confidence among her pupils.

"I had decided to give you three more minutes," she laughed.

"Oh, Miss Tisdale, we'd have been heartbroken if you had gone away without us," exclaimed Jean, as she scrambled into the car.

"No harm done," laughed the teacher.

The car reached the campus gate and slowed down for the turn into Penfield road. Suddenly the girls saw a man step out from behind a stone wall and dart directly into the path of the coupé, holding up his hand.

Miss Tisdale, however, did not stop. She swung the wheel quickly and the car glided

past the stranger. At the same time she spoke
to him tersely through the window:

"Not tonight!"

After a few moments Louise said:

"It's good of you to invite us to meet your
father and mother. They live north of Penfield, don't they?"

"About five miles north," replied Miss Tis-
dale. "I usually go home only week-ends, but
I've been worrying about my father lately, so
I decided to drive out this afternoon."

"Is he ill?" asked Jean quickly.

"He has to be very careful."

Then she began to talk about school matters, and during the journey from Starhurst
to her home Miss Tisdale made no further reference to her parent and made no mention of
the stranger at the campus gate. The Dana
girls realized that she evidently did not care to
discuss these matters with them.

Presently they came within sight of the Tisdale home. It was a spacious white colonial
house, fronted by a well-kept lawn and a box
hedge. Before they could express their ad-
miration of the house and its grounds, while
the coupé was speeding up the cinder roadway,
Miss Tisdale uttered a gasp of alarm.

"My goodness!" she exclaimed. "He'll kill
himself!"

The reason for her fear was obvious. At
the top of a ladder braced against the eaves-

troughing of the house, an elderly man was standing. Up on the roof were two young laborers. The old gentleman was shouting and waving his arms in a state of great excitement.

"It's Father!" gasped Miss Tisdale.

For a person supposed to be in poor health, Mr. Tisdale was exceedingly active and vigorous just now. The girls could hear him hurling orders at the workmen as he teetered to and fro.

"You're not doing the job right!" he was yelling. "I never saw such sloppy work in all my life. I ought to discharge you. Bring those wires over by the chimney! By the *chimney*, I said! Don't you know what a chimney is?"

Miss Tisdale brought the car to a stop. She was greatly upset.

"He shouldn't do such things," she said nervously. "After what the doctor told him —oh!"

She uttered a little scream, for the ladder had slipped along the eavestrough. Mr. Tisdale, still shouting at the workmen, waved his hands wildly.

"That ladder is going to fall!" cried Louise.

She opened the door of the car and leaped out. Even as she rushed toward the house, she saw the ladder slide to one side. Mr. Tisdale lost his balance, grabbed at the roof, and then gripped the eavestrough just as the rung slid out from beneath his feet. The teacher shrieked. Her father yelled. With a crash the ladder toppled over and fell to the ground. Mr. Tisdale was left hanging to the eavestrough.

"Help!" he roared. "I'll be killed! I can't hold on much longer."

Louise had already reached the spot. In a moment she was joined by Jean and in another instant the Dana girls had the ladder back in position. Mr. Tisdale's wildly kicking feet found the rungs just in time. The old gentleman lost no time in scuttling down the ladder to safety.

"Thanks! Thanks!" he panted. "You saved my life. Never had such a narrow escape. Oh, dear, I'm afraid this will be bad for my heart. Too much excitement. Oh, hello, Amy, my dear. Who are these young ladies? I'm very grateful to them, whoever they are——"

He was a lanky old man with silvery hair. When Miss Tisdale introduced Jean and Louise Dana, he bowed courteously and insisted that they come into the house at once. There the girls were presented to Mrs. Tisdale, a stout, lovable woman with a pleasant face. She was greatly alarmed when she heard of her husband's mishap.

"My dear," she said, "you shouldn't have been up there at all. You know what the doctor said."

"Yes, I know. I know," grumbled the old man. "It's very bad for me. Bad for my heart. I'll probably suffer for it. But when I hire workmen to do a job, I want the job done right. Incompetent idiots, that's what those men are."

"What are they doing?" asked Miss Tisdale.

"We're putting in a burglar alarm system," replied her father.

"Burglar alarm?"

"Yes. Prowlers around here lately. I'm not taking any chances."

The Dana girls noticed that Miss Tisdale appeared greatly worried and disturbed by the news. She questioned her parents closely and learned that on three occasions they had seen strangers on the grounds near the house.

"They won't steal anything here," declared Mr. Tisdale. "That burglar alarm will fix them."

Even as he spoke, Louise happened to turn toward one of the windows overlooking the lawn. Beyond the curtains she saw a man's face. It was there for only an instant, then it vanished.

Louise was shaken. Her first impulse was to tell the Tisdales. No one but herself had seen the apparition. Then, on second thought, she decided to say nothing, as she did not want to cause undue alarm to her friends.

The visit could scarcely have been termed a

success. Mrs. Tisdale did what she could to make her guests feel at home, but when dinner was served her husband dominated the table. Never was there such a grouchy and cantankerous old gentleman.

"I'm afraid I'm not long for this world," he moaned. "My health is bad. I'm getting worse every day. I'm liable to drop dead any time."

He was displeased with the soup. He found fault with the roast. He declared that the pudding would give him indigestion. Poor Mrs. Tisdale did her best to enliven the occasion, and her daughter tried to turn the conversation into more cheerful channels, but her father refused to listen.

Immediately after dinner the teacher explained that they would have to return to Starhurst at once. Jean and Louise, knowing that she had planned to spend the evening at home, realized that Miss Tisdale was trying to save them from further embarrassment. The girls felt sorry for her.

"Well, goodbye, Amy," said Mr. Tisdale. "I'm glad you came, even if it was for only a couple of hours. Every time you go away, I feel that I'll never see you again."

"Oh, don't say that, Father."

The kindly Mrs. Tisdale cordially invited the girls to come again, and accompanied them all to the door.

"You'll be home for the week-end, Amy?"
she asked anxiously.

"Yes, Mother. I'll be home on Friday."

While they were driving back to the school,
Miss Tisdale apologized for her father's be-
havior.

"I'm very sorry your visit was disappointing," she said in conclusion.

"Oh, but it wasn't," they protested.

"I know it was. I do wish Father wouldn't
talk so much about his health. Of course, he
really isn't well, and the doctor says that any
sudden shock might kill him."

After this she became very quiet and did not
say another word until Starhurst was reached.

"It's a shame," declared Jean, as the girls
were preparing for bed later, "that Miss Tisdale seems so unhappy. She's about the nicest
teacher here."

"She certainly has been sweet to me," commented Louise, "giving me extra time on those
things I was writing. With her encourage-
ment I believe I might even publish a story
some day—maybe a mystery story."

Jean laughed.

"I haven't forgotten her bravery in the
woods, either, that day we had the picnic," she
reminisced. "Do you recall how she killed
that poisonous snake just when it was going
to strike?"

"Yes, I do, and how kind she was to Lettie," put in Louise, "even when that snob lost her head and threw the whole group into a panic."

"It's a perfect shame such a lovely person has to have so much trouble," sighed Jean.

"It's her home life, I suppose," answered Louise. "She must be dreadfully worried about her father."

Jean was thoughtful.

"She seemed different today. She wasn't nearly as cheerful as usual when we were driving out to her home. Right from the minute we met that man at the gate——"

Louise looked at her sister.

"Do you mean you think that might have had something to do with it?"

"Well, it was odd, don't you think? I wonder what the man wanted."

"All in all," observed Louise, "I think there is some mystery about Miss Tisdale."

"She does act as if she had some great secret on her mind," agreed Jean.

Anything in the way of a mystery always intrigued the Dana girls. They had some talent as amateur detectives, and all Starhurst had recently buzzed with their adventures following the theft of a study lamp presented to them by their Uncle Ned. The story of this strange affair has already been related in the first volume of this series, *By the Light of the Study Lamp*.

The suggestion that Miss Tisdale might be involved in a mystery returned vividly to Jean's mind two days later. It was Friday afternoon, while she was in English class, with the lovable teacher presiding.

"Although he wrote many books," the teacher was saying, "Charles Dickens created his masterpiece when he wrote *David Copperfield*. The book is crowded with characters who will remain immortal as long as the English language is spoken. It is one of the finest bits of fiction——"

At this moment there was a knock at the classroom door and Zeke Daly, the school porter, entered. He shuffled across the room and handed Miss Tisdale a note, then shuffled out again.

The teacher quietly excused herself to the class and opened the note. She read it and then looked up, her face suddenly turning pale.

"Please—go on with your reading assignment for today," she faltered. "You must excuse me." With that she hurried from the room.

There was much whispered speculation among the girls. Jean, who was sitting beside a window, recalled Louise's remark to the effect that there was some mystery about Miss Tisdale. She wondered if the note had anything to do with the stranger they had encountered at the gate.

Idly she looked out across the campus where the dead leaves lay thick on the grass. To her surprise she saw her favorite teacher, hatless, running across the grounds. As the young woman neared the gate, Jean noticed a flat white object flutter from her hand, then she was gone.

"Perhaps something has happened to Mr. Tisdale!" mused Jean.

The moment the English class was over, Jean spoke to Louise and expressed her fear that the instructor had received bad news from home. They were so concerned that they sought out Mrs. Crandall, headmistress of Starhurst, and asked her. The principal, however, had no information.

"I'm sure Miss Tisdale would have told me if anything had happened to her father. She didn't leave any word."

Next morning the affair of the beloved English teacher took a surprising turn. The Dana girls were summoned to Mrs. Crandall's office immediately after breakfast.

"You were asking me about Miss Tisdale yesterday," the headmistress said. "I have just received a telephone call from her mother, who is greatly worried."

"Why, what has happened?" asked Louise quickly.

"Miss Tisdale has disappeared," was the reply.

CHAPTER II

The Empty Coupé

"Miss Tisdale has disappeared?" exclaimed Jean. "What could have happened?"

"Her mother told me," said Mrs. Crandall, "that her daughter had not come home yesterday, and that she had had no word from her."

"Has no one seen her since she left the school yesterday afternoon?" asked Louise.

"I don't believe so," went on Mrs. Crandall. "It's very strange. If she doesn't show up soon, I'll be tempted to turn the matter over to the police."

"Please let us do what we can," Jean begged. "We think a great deal of Miss Tisdale."

"I don't want to call the police to Starhurst unless it's absolutely necessary," said the principal. "Perhaps you girls can help. Mrs. Tisdale seems to have heard of your propensities as amateur detectives, and she requested that I ask you to aid in locating the teacher."

"We'll do our best to trace her," promised Louise eagerly.

"But do not neglect your studies," warned

the headmistress. "And I cannot allow you to become involved in anything dangerous."

Although the Danas assured Mrs. Crandall that their marks would keep up to standard, and that they would be mindful of school rules, they were already turning over in their minds the exciting mystery which they had just heard. As they left the office, Jean took hold of her sister's arm and hurried her along, saying:

"When Miss Tisdale received the note yesterday, she left the school in a hurry. She didn't even wait to get her hat."

"Meaning," declared Louise, "either that she did not expect to be away very long, or that it was an emergency call of some kind.

"First of all," she added, "who sent the note? Perhaps Zeke Daly can tell us something about that. He delivered the message to the classroom, you said."

"Better still," exclaimed Jean with a sudden recollection of the previous afternoon, "we may be able to find the note."

Quickly she explained to Louise that as she had seen Miss Tisdale hurrying across the campus, she had noticed something white flutter from the teacher's hand.

"She was near the gate at the time," said Jean. "If it was the note she dropped, and if we find it, we may learn where she went."

The girls lost no time in leaving the building

and hastening across the campus in the direction taken by Miss Tisdale. They scanned the ground closely, realizing that the wind might have carried the white object a considerable distance since the day before.

"I haven't much hope of finding it," confessed Louise. "And perhaps it wasn't the note after all."

Luck, however, was with them. Jean caught sight of a scrap of white paper lying in the weeds at the base of the campus wall. With a cry of delight she snatched it up. It was damp with dew, and almost fell apart as Jean with trembling fingers unfolded it.

"Is it the note?" cried Louise excitedly.

Five words were typewritten on the paper. When the girls read them, they had little doubt but that this was the message Miss Tisdale had received. Yet the contents, instead of helping them, mystified them all the more, for the words were:

"Faith gone. Come at once."

No name was signed to this strange summons.

"What can it mean?" asked Louise.

"It must have meant a great deal to Miss Tisdale. She turned deathly pale when she read that note."

"Who gave the message to Zeke Daly in the first place? That's the point," said Louise.

They found Zeke Daly burning rubbish at

the back of the school. He was an elderly, stoop-shouldered man, somewhat deaf. When the girls asked him about the note he cupped his hand to his ear and shouted "Hey?"

"It's about the note! The note you gave Miss Tisdale," cried Jean.

"Boat?"

"No. Not boat. Note!"

"What note?" bellowed Zeke.

"The note you gave Miss Tisdale!"

Zeke scratched his head thoughtfully.

"Oh, yes. *That* note. What about it?"

"Who gave it to you?"

Zeke raked a few leaves onto the rubbish pile.

"Man in a car," he said finally.

"Where was he?" asked Jean.

"What did he look like?" demanded Louise.

"Don't shout," advised Zeke. "I can hear you. I'm not deaf. What did you say?"

"Where was he and what did he look like?" cried Jean in exasperation.

Zeke thought it over before answering. Finally he said:

"Well, he come along in a car and stopped near the gate. He called me over and asked me to give a note to Miss Tisdale. And by the time she come out he'd gone away."

"What did he look like?"

"Well—he might have been a short fellow and he might have been a tall fellow. I dunno, seein' as he was sittin' in the car. Just an ordinary-lookin' fellow.''

"What color was his hair?" asked Louise.

"He had his hat on," grunted Zeke. "Just an ordinary-lookin' hat."

"My, but you're helpful," sighed Jean.

Zeke did not hear her and went on talking.

"So when Miss Tisdale run out to the gate and found he was gone, she went back to the garage and got her own car."

"Which way did she go?" the girls demanded.

Zeke gestured toward the south.

"Down that way. She couldn't have gone very far, though. Didn't have much gas. She asked me to fill up the tank the night before. I forgot."

This was all the information they could glean from Zeke, but it was sufficient to establish two important facts. Miss Tisdale had gone south, and she had gone in her own car. This gave Louise an idea.

"What we must do now," she declared, "is to call at all the gas stations along the south road."

"Yes," agreed her sister, "she would have had to stop for fuel sooner or later."

The girls knew that there was such a place about half a mile down the road, so they set out at once. They realized that their chances of tracing the car were slim if Miss Tisdale had continued along the main road. However, Louise argued that if the teacher had stopped along the way, it was possible that she might have dropped some hint as to her destination.

A young man in overalls grinned cheerfully at them as they approached the gas station.

"Hello, girls! Out for a hike?"

"We're trying to trace a car," replied Louise.

"You'll never catch up to it on foot," retorted the attendant.

"Maybe not," laughed Jean. "Were you on duty yesterday afternoon at about three o'clock? We're trying to trace a blue coupé, driven by a lady——"

"Blue coupé. Driven by a lady. Correct," said the young man. "I saw it. The car stalled a couple of hundred yards from here. Out of gas."

"Which way did she go?"

"She left the main road at the first turn," the station attendant told them. "She went down that wood road to the left. You can see it from here."

"The road to Hilton!" said Jean.

"The lady seemed to be in a hurry to get to Hilton—of all places in this world. I can imagine people being in a hurry to get *away* from Hilton, but hurrying to get there—no!"

"Thank you," said Louise. "You've helped us a great deal."

The girls went on their way, delighted that they had made better progress than they had expected.

"She probably went farther than Hilton, though," said Jean. "That's only a tiny village."

However, they entered the winding road that led from the main highway and patiently trudged along. The route was bordered by a rail fence almost hidden by high bushes.

"Listen!" commanded Jean suddenly, when they had gone a few hundred yards.

The girls stopped. From a distance came a plaintive cry.

"I thought so," said Jean. "It is a child."

The sound was repeated, and this time there was no chance of mistaking its origin. Somewhere beyond the bushes a little one was weeping as if heartbroken.

"Probably lost," reflected Louise.

They scrambled over the fence and forced their way through the underbrush. There, in a clearing, they found a golden-haired little girl sobbing pitifully. Her pretty face was stained with tears, and she was trembling with fear. The moment she saw the girls she doubled her sobs and stumbled toward them.

"I'se losted!" she wept, rubbing her eyes with a grubby little fist.

"You poor darling!" said Louise, picking the tot up in her arms. "You're lost, are you?

Well, never mind. We'll bring you home again. Where do you live?"

The little girl was about five years old. She was so forlorn and frightened that the girls' hearts went out to her. It was some time before she stopped crying. Jean dried the child's eyes with her handkerchief.

"Now," she said briskly, "where do you live?"

"Wiv Muvver."

"Who is Mother?"

"Why—why—she's just Muvver."

"Well, where does *she* live?" asked Louise.

"At our house," replied the child. "In Hilton."

"Well, that isn't very far away," said Jean. "What's your name?"

"Muvver calls me Baby Fa-ab."

"All right, Fa-ab," laughed Louise. "We'll bring you back to your mother."

Jean noticed a trail leading from the clearing. "Did you come from Hilton by the road, Fa-ab?"

The child pointed to the trail.

"I walked," she said, "an' walked, an' walked. Then I got losted."

"That path is a short cut to Hilton. I imagine," Louise suggested. "We'll follow it, anyway."

They struck out, Louise carrying the little girl, and in a few minutes they emerged from

the woods on the edge of a small settlement.
There they saw an anxious woman scurrying
about, obviously looking for someone, and they
at once assumed that she was the child's
mother. When she saw the girls approaching,
she ran toward them.

"Thank goodness!" exclaimed the woman, a
sharp-featured housewife with stringy black
hair. "I just missed her this minute. I was
looking high and low."

"We found her up near the woods road," explained Louise. "She was lost. All right,
Fa-ab. Here you are, back with your mother
again."

"That's not Muvver," said the child indig-
nantly.

"Indeed, and I'm not," the woman said. "I
was just minding her, as if I hadn't enough to
do, what with children of my own and the Sat-
urday baking. Her mother lives across the
street."

She indicated a little brown-shingled cottage
on the other side of the road. It was set back
on a rise of ground, and its entrance was completely hidden by a huge pine, the only tree
near the tiny house.

"Her mother had to go to see the doctor, and
she asked me to mind the little girl while she
was gone," went on the woman. "I like to be
neighborly, but I have enough to do looking
after my own youngsters. Besides, it isn't as

if she's the kind of person you like to do favors for. I believe in neighbors bein' neighbors, but *her*—my goodness, you'd think she was doing us all a favor by living in Hilton at all. Keeps to herself like the Queen of Egypt, she does, and close-mouthed. You can never get a word out of her."

The woman evidently had small regard for Baby Fa-ab's mother.

"She won't hold her head so high one of these days, I'm thinkin'," she declared. "Believe me, all widows who keep their mouths so tight shut have got something to be ashamed of, and the truth will come out sooner or later."

The Dana girls were embarrassed by these confidences. They had no desire to listen to the woman's malicious gossip, so they hurriedly changed the subject.

"By the way," said Jean, "did you see a blue coupé pass through here yesterday afternoon at about half-past three? There was a lady driving."

The woman shook her head.

"Not many cars pass through Hilton," she said. "It's sort of out of the way. No, there was no such car went through yesterday afternoon. I would have seen it."

The Dana girls were disappointed. Their search had ended in a blind alley. If this well-informed woman had not seen the car pass through Hilton, then it was probable that it had not.

"We had better go back," said Jean. "The auto may have gone down a side road."

"All that walk for nothing," grumbled Jean.

"I shouldn't say it was for nothing," replied Louise. "I'm glad we found that poor child. Her mother would have been greatly worried."

"That's true," admitted Jean. "And wasn't the little girl darling? I wonder what her mother is like. She must not lead a very pleasant existence with that gossipy woman spying on her from across the street all the time."

The girls decided to follow the woods road instead of taking the short cut back to the place where they had found the lost child. As events later proved, this was a momentous decision, for after walking a short distance they saw a car in the ditch some distance ahead of them.

"That auto looks familiar," said Louise suddenly.

"It's a blue coupé!" cried Jean.

The girls broke into a run. In a few minutes they reached the car and recognized it instantly.

"Miss Tisdale's coupé!" exclaimed Louise. "It's been abandoned here by the roadside."

The Dana girls had found the teacher's car. But where was Miss Tisdale?

CHAPTER III

The Mysterious Sailor

Jean and Louise hastily searched the abandoned automobile. On the floor they found one of Miss Tisdale's calling cards. This was enough to convince them that they had made no mistake in identifying the coupé as that of the English teacher.

The key was still in the ignition. Two wheels of the car were deeply embedded in the mud of the ditch. Louise expressed the opinion that the machine had been standing there for some time.

"Look!" exclaimed Louise. "There are double sets of tire marks on the road. The coupé was evidently forced into the ditch by another car."

A comparison of the two different imprints supported Louise's contention. Jean then discovered that the mud immediately beside Miss Tisdale's coupé had been disturbed and heavily trodden upon with so many footprints, that it was impossible to distinguish one from another.

"There has been a struggle of some sort,"

23

she said. Suddenly she reached into the tall grass at the edge of the ditch as a gleaming object caught her eye.

"A wrist watch!" she gasped, snatching it up.

The girls examined the bit of jewelry.

"Miss Tisdale's watch!" whispered Louise in awe.

They saw that the catch was broken.

"Her car was forced off the road by another car," said Jean. "The other car stopped. There are marks of a struggle. We find Miss Tisdale's broken wrist watch. Her car has been abandoned here since late yesterday afternoon, because the hood is pointing toward Hilton and she never reached Hilton. It can mean only one thing."

"That she was forced into the other car and taken away," added Louise.

"But why?"

"I can't even guess the reason. But I *do* know we had better report this to Mrs. Crandall at once. We'll drive the car back to Starhurst."

They got into the coupé. Louise took the wheel and, after considerable difficulty, managed to get the car out of the ditch and up onto the road. Then swiftly they drove back toward Penfield.

The discovery they had made frightened them. Had Miss Tisdale been lured into a trap through the strange message she had received? And why had she been spirited away in this manner?

Mrs. Crandall was shocked beyond words when the girls returned to the school and hastily told her what they had discovered. She frowned in deep perplexity as she considered the problem.

"I can't understand it," she said. "I do hope there is some happy explanation for this strange happening. And yet, as you say, it isn't likely that Miss Tisdale would stay away without sending word to us if she could possibly do so."

"And she wouldn't deliberately abandon her car in a ditch," Jean pointed out.

"It is all very, very queer," agreed Mrs. Crandall. "Of course, Mrs. Tisdale must be informed of this at once," she added, reaching for the telephone. "I'm sure I don't relish the task of breaking the news to her, but Mrs. Tisdale will have to know the truth sooner or later."

In a moment she was talking to the mother of the missing teacher. Gently Mrs. Crandall explained that the Dana girls had discovered Miss Tisdale's car.

"I do not think there is anything seriously wrong, Mrs. Tisdale. My own advice would be to inform the police——"

From the telephone the girls overheard a

sharp interruption. Mrs. Crandall listened attentively.

"I understand," she said at last. "Yes—yes—the Dana girls?—Why, I'm sure they'll be glad to help you if they can·—I see—very well, Mrs. Tisdale, I shall respect your wishes. We'll let you know if we hear of any developments."

She replaced the receiver and turned to the sisters.

"Mrs. Tisdale begged me to ask you to go on with the search. Really, it is pathetic the way she puts so much confidence in you. She says she does not dare inform the police of the matter because Mr. Tisdale might hear of it."

"She doesn't want him to know?" exclaimed Louise in surprise.

"Evidently not. She was most emphatic on that point. I imagine she is afraid it might have a bad effect on his heart. She also asked me to tell you to use Miss Tisdale's coupé whenever you wish. And she would like to see you early this afternoon."

"We'll drive over to her home directly after luncheon," said Louise.

"Very well. But I still think Mrs. Tisdale should notify the police," observed Mrs. Crandall as she brought the interview to a close.

"Mrs. Crandall doesn't think much of our ability as detectives," laughed Jean as they went down the hall.

"I think myself it is really a case for the police," remarked Louise seriously.

The school was already buzzing with rumors about the strange disappearance of the English teacher, and many of the girls had seen the Dana sisters arriving at Starhurst in Miss Tisdale's coupé. When they went up to their study, they found Evelyn Starr and a number of other classmates waiting eagerly for news.

Their story created an immediate sensation. The room was a babel of excited voices. Starhurst had not known such a tempest since the affair of the missing study lamp.

Suddenly, while all the students were trying to talk at once, a harsh voice broke in.

"Mystery! I never heard such nonsense. There's no mystery about it."

A silence fell over the room. Then the assembled group looked up to see Lettie Briggs standing in the doorway. Behind her lurked Ina Mason, her only friend, a meek, toadying person who was apparently willing to sacrifice any pride she had for the sake of being known as the chum of the richest girl at Starhurst.

"If there isn't any mystery," said Louise, "perhaps you can explain the disappearance to us, Lettie."

"Of course I can explain it," snapped the girl. "Miss Tisdale has eloped with the man she has been meeting downtown. That's all there is to it."

Then, apparently satisfied that she had exploded a bombshell and created an impression, Lettie Briggs swept down the hall toward her own study.

Evelyn Starr whistled softly.

"This *is* news!" she exclaimed. "I didn't know Miss Tisdale had an admirer."

"News to me, too," declared Jean. "I'm going to find out about this," she added, as she left the study and went in pursuit of Lettie Briggs.

"Surprised you, didn't I?" exclaimed the haughty girl when Jean tapped at the half open door and came into the study. "Thought you were going to have another mystery to solve, didn't you?"

"Well, it will be a mystery until Miss Tisdale is found," said Jean.

"Nothing of the sort," scoffed Lettie.

"You say she was meeting someone? What did he look like?"

Lettie regarded Jean haughtily.

"I never thought you would condescend to ask *me* for information," she replied disagreeably. "However, if you're very much interested I don't mind telling you. I've seen her with him several times. Once in front of the Regal Restaurant, and two or three times in front of the Continental House. He was a tall man, dark, and very handsome. Oh, he was her boy friend all right. Why, the last time I saw them together he seemed to be proposing to her.''

"That's so," chimed in Ina Mason. "Tall and dark and handsome.''

"Anything else you want to know?" demanded Lettie.

"No thanks," replied Jean, and withdrew, closing the door behind her.

Thoughtfully she went back down the hall. Lettie's story had brought to light a new angle of the disappearance of Miss Tisdale. Nevertheless, Jean somehow felt that the tale did not ring true. On a sudden inspiration she turned and retraced her steps, tiptoeing along the hall. Outside Lettie's door she stopped and listened.

"That ought to put those snoopy Danas off the track," she heard Lettie saying.

"Tall and dark and handsome," snickered Ina. "Oh, I could have laughed right out loud when you told her that.''

"If there's a mystery to be solved, we'll do it," declared Lettie. "We'll show them that other girls in this school are just as smart as that pair. Yes, I think we put them off the track that time."

"The stranger was anything but handsome," said Ina.

"He was positively homely. Short and kind of fat, and seemed something like a sailor."

Ina giggled shrilly.

"The Danas will be looking all over for a dark, handsome man when they should be trying to locate a short, fat sailor."

Jean had heard enough. She smiled to herself as she went quietly back to her friends. When the other girls had left the Dana study, she immediately told Louise of her interview with Lettie Briggs and of what she had later overheard.

"It's a good joke on Lettie," said Jean. "She really gave us some valuable information after all. We now know that Miss Tisdale has been meeting a sailor in Penfield."

This information was uppermost in their minds when they drove out early that afternoon to see Mrs. Tisdale. She met them as they walked up the steps to the veranda.

"Do come in," she said in an agitated voice. She glanced nervously over her shoulder, and then whispered: "Mr. Tisdale doesn't know anything about it. He mustn't find out what has happened."

The nervous woman escorted the girls into a front room and carefully closed the door. Then she collapsed wearily into a chair and began to cry.

"Oh, what has happened to Amy?" she sobbed. "This suspense is dreadful. I'm so worried and upset——"

The Dana girls did their best to comfort her.

"She'll come back, never fear," Louise as

sured her sympathetically. "We'll do all we can to help you."

Mrs. Tisdale dried her eyes.

"Please tell me all about it," she begged. "You found her car, didn't you? Ever since Mrs. Crandall told me she was missing, I've been almost wild with anxiety. I haven't dared tell Mr. Tisdale a thing."

"Is it because you are afraid the shock might harm him?" asked Louise.

"Well, yes—partly that," admitted Mrs. Tisdale. "He mustn't know about it."

"Did your daughter have any enemies?"

The woman shook her head.

"I'm sure Amy hadn't an enemy in the world," she insisted. "She is so kind and friendly, she was on good terms with everybody she knew."

"Did she have a sailor friend?" asked Louise.

Mrs. Tisdale looked at the girls in surprise.

"A sailor?" she exclaimed. "Why, no. I never heard Amy speak of any sailors."

The girls were disappointed. They had hoped that Mrs. Tisdale might have been able to help them learn more about the man her daughter had met in Penfield.

"I'm sure she didn't know any sailors," repeated Mrs. Tisdale. "But I can tell you something in confidence. It may have had something to do with her disappearance."

CHAPTER IV

LONE TREE COTTAGE

"WE CAN keep a secret," promised Jean, when Mrs. Tisdale offered to tell the Dana girls something in confidence. Louise echoed her sister's sentiments.

"Amy has a twin sister," began Mrs. Tisdale in a hushed voice and with another nervous glance at the hall door.

"A twin sister!" they exclaimed in surprise.

"She never mentioned her to us," said Louise.

"Well—you see," faltered the woman, "Amy's sister hasn't been inside this house for years. It's a family secret. Mr. Tisdale won't allow her name to be mentioned in his presence."

She dabbed at her eyes with her handkerchief.

"Oh, dear," she said with a catch in her voice, "I've lost one daughter—and now the other is gone."

"Where is the twin sister living?" Jean asked.

"I don't know. She left home several years

32

ago. She had a quarrel with her father because she wanted to marry a man named Brixton, and Mr. Tisdale didn't approve of him. So she eloped, and that's the last we ever saw of her. Mr. Tisdale was dreadfully angry. He gave orders that I was never to speak of her again.''

A frightened look crossed her face. She put a finger to her lips.

"Not a word!'' she cautioned.

Outside the door they heard halting footsteps, then a muttering and grumbling. Finally the knob turned, and then old Mr. Tisdale stumped in.

"Why do you sit in here with the door closed?'' he barked angrily. "Never saw such a woman—oh!''

Suddenly he realized that his wife was entertaining company. He stared at the Dana girls.

"Oh, hello!'' he snapped. "You're the girls who were here the other day. How are you? Don't tell me. I know. You're feeling fine. Well, I'm not. I never felt worse. Never felt worse in my life.''

The girls had the impression that he felt proud of it.

"Can't find my dyspepsia tablets,'' he shouted at his wife. "Where are they? I've looked high and low for them.''

"I'll get them for you, John,'' said Mrs.

Tisdale meekly, as she flashed the girls a warning glance.

"I think we'll have to go now," said Louise, rising. "We just dropped in for a little chat."

"Well, stop in any time," invited Mr. Tisdale. "Any time at all. It's a pleasure to see young people around the house. Healthy young people. Dear me, though, nobody appreciates health nowadays. Nobody appreciates good health until he's lost it."

As the girls were driving back to Starhurst, they discussed Mrs. Tisdale's interesting story of the twin sister. However, they were not inclined to believe that this family secret had anything to do with the teacher's mysterious disappearance.

"It all happened several years ago," Louise pointed out. "The sister is probably living hundreds of miles away from here. Moreover, I can't see why anyone should want to take Miss Tisdale away as a result of that affair."

Nevertheless, it was one of the few occurrences in the missing teacher's life which was out of the ordinary. As such, the girls should consider it in their efforts to solve the mystery.

"Perhaps," suggested Jean, "the sailor she met in Penfield was really Mr. Brixton, her sister's husband."

"It's possible," agreed Louise, "but not probable. If the Brixtons had wanted to get in touch with her, it would have had to be done very quietly because of Mr. Tisdale. But on the other hand, why should the Brixtons have anything to do with Miss Tisdale's disappearance? She might have gone to visit them without saying anything about it to anyone, but would never have left her car standing abandoned by the roadside."

"Let's stop in Penfield and see if we can learn something about this sailor," suggested Jean impulsively. "I think he's at the bottom of the whole situation. Lettie said she saw the sailor and Miss Tisdale near the Regal Restaurant and the Continental House. We can make inquiries there."

"No harm in trying," said Louise. "But I don't believe it will do any good."

However, when they drove into Penfield and sought information about "a short, stout sailor" from the manager of the Continental House, they were pleasantly surprised.

"Why, yes," said the clerk, "there was a man of that description staying here for several days."

"Was his name Brixton?" asked Jean eagerly.

"No. There has been no one by the name of Brixton here. This chap called himself Mr. Tepper. But he does answer your description. Middle-aged man, quite fat, and he dressed somewhat like a sailor. Walked and talked like a seaman, too."

"Is he still here?" asked Louise.

"No, he checked out day before yesterday."

"Did he leave a forwarding address for his mail?" inquired Jean quickly.

"No forwarding address. He didn't say where he was going. As a matter of fact, I don't know where he came from. When he registered he merely wrote 'Sol Tepper—the Seven Seas.' That's all I know about him."

With this meager information the Dana girls were obliged to be satisfied for the time being.

"However," said Louise, "we're making progress. We know more than we did this morning. Let's sum things up. We know that Miss Tisdale received a note——"

"Saying 'Faith gone. Come at once,'" quoted Jean.

"Someone had lost faith in her. The message was typewritten. We know that she was greatly alarmed, that she hurried away and drove toward Hilton in her car. Another machine forced her off the road, there was a struggle, and she was taken away in the second car. We hear she had been meeting a man, presumably a sailor, by the name of Sol Tepper. We also know that she had a twin sister named Mrs. Brixton."

"It's like the unfitted pieces of a jigsaw puzzle," said Jean.

"It's worse than any jigsaw puzzle I ever tried to put together."

"About that note," suggested Jean. "You say it meant that someone had lost faith in her. Perhaps we're on the wrong track altogether. I think the word 'Faith' is somebody's name."

This angle had not occurred to Louise.

"Mrs. Brixton, perhaps!" she exclaimed.

"We should have asked Mrs. Tisdale if her married daughter's name was Faith."

"We'll telephone now and find out," decided Louise.

Before returning to Starhurst they went into a drug store booth where they put through a call. In a few moments Louise heard Mrs. Tisdale's voice on the wire.

"What is it?" asked the anxious woman. "Have you heard any news?"

"Nothing yet, Mrs. Tisdale, I'm sorry to report," Louise answered. "But we're trying to run down a clue. It's about Mrs. Brixton. What is her first name? Is it Faith?"

"Faith?" said Mrs. Tisdale. "No. Her first name is Alice."

Louise was disappointed. Then she had a sudden inspiration.

"Has she any children?"

"If there was a child," answered Mrs. Tisdale, "I have never heard of it."

"Well, then," continued Louise, "could you tell me something about Mr. Brixton? Is he a sailor? A short, stout man?"

"No, Mr. Brixton was never a sailor to my knowledge. And he wasn't short and stout. Just the opposite. Tall and thin."

"Oh, dear," sighed Louise. "I thought we were on the right track, but we've been all wrong."

"I do hope you have some news for me soon," said Mrs. Tisdale. "I'm afraid I haven't been of very much help to you."

"We'll do the very best we can," Louise promised.

She turned ruefully away from the telephone.

"Another setback," she said. "I think the Brixtons are not mixed up in this at all."

This was the situation at the end of the afternoon. Miss Tisdale had disappeared as completely as if the earth had opened and swallowed her up. No word had come from her. Had it not been for the evidence of a struggle in the vicinity of the parked car, the Dana girls would have been inclined to the belief that the teacher had gone away of her own accord. But that explanation was unlikely.

"No," said Louise, as the girls were preparing for bed that evening, "she was taken away. But why?"

"Ransom," was Jean's suggestion.

"Who would pay it?"

"Mr. Tisdale."

"But no message has been received demanding money," Louise pointed out.

"It may not have reached the Tisdales yet."

Next morning, however, Louise had an idea. It had occurred to her that they might have been hasty in returning to Starhurst so soon after discovering Miss Tisdale's car.

"Why was she going toward Hilton?" said Louise. "If we can learn the answer to that question, we'll be on the right track."

"Let's get some horses and ride over there," Jean suggested. "In a small village like Hilton everyone knows everyone else. If Miss Tisdale has been there before, we'll soon find it out."

Immediately after breakfast the Dana girls went down to the stables, where Zeke Daly saddled two handsome mares for them. Soon they were jogging down the highway. No one, seeing the two pretty girls in their neat riding habits, and cantering along to the tune of clattering hoofs this clear, but cold morning, would have thought that they were on an errand of mystery.

They finally reached Hilton. The little village lay quiet and peaceful in the November sunlight. Louise had suggested that they first visit the loquacious woman with whom they had talked the previous day.

"She likes to gossip. She seems to know

everything about everybody in Hilton,'' laughed Louise.

They dismounted in front of the unattractive little house. Three untidy-looking youngsters came tumbling out of the door and stared at the horses. They were followed by their mother, drying her hands on a gingham apron.

"Good morning," said Louise pleasantly. "I hope we're not disturbing you."

"Oh, you're not disturbing *me*," said the woman. "There's little enough ever happens in this place, and it ain't often that anyone stops long enough to have a chat. My, those are nice-looking horses! You girls must be from Starhurst School."

"Yes, we are," replied Jean, smiling. "Do you know Miss Tisdale? She's one of our teachers."

The woman shook her head.

"Miss Tisdale? No, I can't say I know her. Leastways, not by name. There's a teacher from Starhurst comes out here often in a car. Maybe that's her. She visits the woman across the street."

The Dana girls tried to conceal their excitement.

"The mother of the little girl we found near the road yesterday?" asked Louise.

"Yes. Mrs. Brixton is her name. She lives right over there in the house with the pine tree in front of it."

"Mrs. Brixton!" exclaimed Jean. Then, observing that the woman was surprised by her obvious amazement, she said: "The name startled me. Someone was talking to me about a Mrs. Brixton just yesterday."

"No relation, I guess," said the woman. "I'm sure this Mrs. Brixton hasn't any people in these parts. Nor many friends either, except that teacher from Starhurst. Can't expect to have many friends when you keep to yourself the way she does. That widow," declared the woman confidentially, "has a *past!* I know it. Never saw such a close-mouthed neighbor in all my born days."

Shrewishly she voiced her opinion that Mrs. Brixton was living under a cloud.

"It'll all come out some day, though. She won't hold her head so high then. She's no better than anybody else, and if the truth was known, I guess she isn't as good as most."

The Dana girls were obliged to listen to her vindictive gossip for some time. At last, however, making an excuse to the effect that they wanted to see "Baby Fa-ab," they managed to get away.

"Do you know," whispered Jean, as they crossed the road, "I have an idea!"

"What is it?"

"I think Baby Fa-ab is Baby Faith. That's the child's way of saying her own name. The word 'Faith' in that note meant the child."

"But the message said, 'Faith gone,' and the child wasn't gone," objected Louise.

Jean had no answer to make to this. Nevertheless, she was still convinced that the name in the note bore some sort of reference to Mrs. Brixton's little daughter.

As the girls went up the path toward the tiny brown-shingled cottage, they were very much impressed by the aloofness of the place. The tall pine tree towered far above the house, its branches reaching out like long arms into the sky. There was no sound save that made by the creaking of the boughs, as the brisk wind played against the long green needles.

"Lone Tree Cottage!" remarked Louise. "Sounds just like the kind of place for a deep secret."

They rapped at the door, and presently it opened slowly. A young woman confronted them. She was pale and slight, with a sad, careworn face and tragic eyes. But her resemblance to Miss Tisdale was so startling that the Dana girls unwittingly gasped.

There was no doubt in their minds but that she was the twin sister of the missing teacher.

"How do you do?" said the woman in a quiet voice.

"You are Mrs. Brixton?" asked Louise.

"Yes."

"My name is Louise Dana. This is my sister Jean. We are from Starhurst School."

"Yes?"

"Aren't you the sister of one of our teachers —Miss Tisdale?"

Mrs. Brixton looked suddenly frightened. Then, with an obvious effort, she collected herself.

"Miss Tisdale?" she asked, as if she had never before heard the name. "I'm afraid you have made a mistake in coming here. I must bid you good morning."

With these words she made a motion as if to close the door.

CHAPTER V

A Strange Confession

WHEN Jean saw that the widow was determined not to admit the relationship, she spoke up quickly.

"We had hoped you might be able to give us some information. Miss Tisdale has disappeared——"

Mrs. Brixton uttered a cry of alarm, clutching her throat with her hands.

"What's that?" she demanded. "Amy has disappeared? What do you mean?"

"Then you *are* her sister!" exclaimed Louise.

"Yes. Yes," replied the young woman nervously. "But what do you mean by saying she has disappeared?"

"She left Starhurst day before yesterday in the afternoon, intending to come here," explained Louise, "and she hasn't been seen since."

Mrs. Brixton clung to the door for support. Her face went white. The girls thought for a moment she was going to faint. Then she broke into a wild fit of hysterical weeping.

"Oh, I didn't know! I didn't know!" she cried. "She must be found——"

Her nerves gave way. She ran back into the hall, still crying, calling out her sister's name time and again. In a moment she burst into uncontrollable laughter, which was followed by another fit of weeping.

Suddenly there was a dull thud. Then silence.

"She has fainted!" cried Louise.

She rushed into the house. Jean followed, closing the door behind her. They found Mrs. Brixton lying unconscious on the floor. Baby Faith toddled in from the kitchen, gazed in wonder at her mother, then began to cry in terror.

The girls lifted up the young widow and placed her upon a couch in the living room. Louise tried to comfort Baby Faith, while Jean ran to the kitchen for water. In a few minutes they managed to revive the stricken woman, who opened her eyes and tossed wretchedly on the couch.

"Amy must be found!" she moaned. "She must be found! Oh, it's all my fault."

It was some time before she was calm enough to talk coherently. Then, drying her eyes, she slowly raised herself from the couch.

"You must excuse me for giving way like this," said Mrs. Brixton. "I'm afraid I was very rude in not admitting that Amy is my sister. But I've had to be so careful. Please tell me all that has happened."

The girls then related to her the story of Miss Tisdale's disappearance, explaining how they had traced the car and had found it abandoned on the road outside Hilton.

"Then she must have been on her way here!" said the widow. "She often drove out from Starhurst to see me. But what could have happened? Why should anyone have taken her away? I cannot understand it."

"We have been talking to your mother," explained Louise, "and she has asked us to do what we can toward finding your sister."

"Does my father know about it?" asked Mrs. Brixton suddenly.

"Your mother insisted that the news be kept from him," Jean said.

"And you mustn't tell him about me," pleaded the widow. "You mustn't tell Mother, either. You see, they don't know I'm living here. It's a long story," said Mrs. Brixton. "I'm in disgrace at home—because I married a man to whom my father objected."

"Mrs. Tisdale mentioned something about it," observed Louise quietly.

"My husband died, leaving me with Baby Faith," continued the young widow. "He passed away suddenly, and there was very little money for us. He carried no insurance. I was living in Florida at the time, and didn't dare write home for help, because my father had disowned me when I had gone away to get married.''

''Why didn't you write to your mother?'' asked Jean sympathetically.

''She would have had to have gone to Father for the money and given him a reason. So that was out of the question. There was only one person to whom I could turn for help, and that was my twin sister, Amy.''

''And she helped you?''

''She couldn't ask Father for money, of course, but she did everything she could for me. That is why she accepted the position at Starhurst.''

The Dana girls now understood why Miss Tisdale had been teaching, in spite of the fact that her parents were comparatively wealthy.

''She told them that she wanted to go to work,'' Mrs. Brixton went on. ''I would have gone to work myself, but I was ill and couldn't leave Faith. She was only a baby. Amy was a darling and sent me all the money she could spare. Even so, it has been a struggle, for a great many dollars have gone to doctors. I haven't been in good health for some time. I came up here and rented this cottage so I could be near Amy, but of course she didn't let my parents know.''

''Have you any idea,'' asked Louise, ''why anyone should want to take Miss Tisdale away?

She was evidently on her way here when her car was forced off the road.''

"I haven't the faintest idea!" said Mrs. Brixton sadly. "She had no enemies, as far as I know. For that matter, she had very few close friends.''

"Did she ever mention a man by the name of Mr. Tepper?" asked Jean, thinking of the sailor whom Miss Tisdale had met in Penfield.

A startled light flashed into the widow's eyes.

"Tepper!" she exclaimed. "Is he——?"

Then she checked herself. Apparently it occurred to her that she should not confide too freely in these girls who were, after all, total strangers to her.

"Why do you ask about him?" she said, cautiously.

"Because we think he may have had something to do with the disappearance of your sister," Louise promptly replied. "We're trying to help you and your mother. You see, Jean and I once solved a mystery at Starhurst, and Miss Tisdale told your mother about it. She seems to think we might be of help to her in this case. We're only too willing to do the best we possibly can.''

Mrs. Brixton appeared satisfied by this explanation of their interest in the affair.

"I recall now that Amy mentioned your names. It was something about a study lamp, wasn't it? I'll be glad to tell you anything I know. But first of all, where did you ever hear about Mr. Tepper?''

The girls explained how they had learned of Miss Tisdale's meetings with the man in Penfield.

"Yes," said Mrs. Brixton, "that would be Sol Tepper. He used to be a sailor. He was my husband's partner.''

"His business partner?" asked Jean.

"Yes. My husband and Tepper owned a company for manufacturing life preservers. I never liked Mr. Tepper. He came to our house a few times when my husband was alive. I'm sure he is a rascal, because after Mr. Brixton died Mr. Tepper told me that the business had been a failure, and that no money was due my husband's estate from the company. I believe he was telling an untruth, because Mr. Brixton always led me to believe that the business was profitable, but I couldn't prove anything. Then, a few weeks ago, Mr. Tepper located me here. He actually came to this house.''

"But why?" demanded Jean.

"Asking for money. This time he claimed that my husband had stolen a sum from him. He insinuated that I had the money, and he said he wanted it.''

"You didn't give it to him, I hope?" Louise exclaimed.

Mrs. Brixton smiled faintly.

"Even if I had believed him, I couldn't have given him anything. I told him that my sister was supporting me. But that was a bad move."

"He didn't go to Miss Tisdale?"

"Yes," said the widow. "He went to Amy and demanded five thousand dollars. That was the amount he said my husband had stolen from him. There isn't a word of truth in the whole story, I'm sure, and under any other circumstances we would have told him to take his claim to court and prove it. But we couldn't do that and he knew it."

"Why?" asked Jean.

"Because my father would then hear the whole story. Amy has told me that he is in very poor health and that a sudden shock might kill him. Tepper knew this. He also realized that he held the upper hand because he was aware of our secret. He threatened to go to my father and tell him the whole story unless we gave him the money he demanded."

The Dana girls looked at each other in dismay. They now knew the reason for Miss Tisdale being so worried and preoccupied in the weeks preceding her disappearance. Tepper's demands amounted to blackmail.

"But why didn't he go to your father when he failed to receive the money?" asked Louise.

"Amy didn't actually refuse him. She didn't dare to do that. I think she was hoping against hope that she would be able to discourage him in some way. She kept putting him off, without actually telling him that she couldn't give him the money. But now—well, I'm sure Tepper must be at the bottom of the whole affair. I think he has carried off Amy, perhaps in the hope of forcing her to get the money which he demands."

The girls were deeply moved by Mrs. Brixton's story. They were also excited because they knew that they had made a decided advance in their efforts to solve the mystery of Miss Tisdale's disappearance. In the activities of Tepper, the former sailor and ex-partner of Mr. Brixton, doubtless lay the solution.

"What I can't understand," said Mrs. Brixton, "is how Amy came to be led into the trap. She was always very cautious in her dealings with Tepper, because she knew he couldn't be trusted."

"He must have known, somehow, that you wrote her that note asking her to come and see you," suggested Jean.

Mrs. Brixton was surprised.

"I didn't write her a note!" she exclaimed.

Louise quickly took a paper from her pocket.

"We found this near the campus gate," she said. "Miss Tisdale dropped it when she left the school. Look—it's typewritten and it asks her to come at once."

Mrs. Brixton looked at the soiled and crumpled scrap of paper.

"No! No!" she cried. "I didn't write that. We always wrote to each other in code. But it's my typewriter!"

The strain was too much for her. She uttered a low moan and then sank back on the couch. She had fainted again.

CHAPTER VI

THE SECRET WORDS

THE girls revived Mrs. Brixton with difficulty. As it was obvious that the young widow was in need of medical attention, Louise took the liberty of telephoning to Penfield for a doctor. They were afraid that the effects of strain and shock might prove serious. Mrs. Brixton protested, but the Dana girls had their way. When the physician arrived, about twenty minutes later, he approved their judgment.

"You shouldn't be on your feet at all," he told Mrs. Brixton. "You're badly run down and you'll have to take care of yourself. You must go to bed and stay there."

"But I can't afford to engage a nurse," cried Mrs. Brixton. "Who will look after the house? Who will take care of Baby Faith?"

At this moment the front door opened. The talkative neighbor woman, seeing the doctor's car in front of the house, had been unable to curb her impatience.

"What's the matter here?" she demanded briskly.

The doctor explained. The neighbor woman,

53

who introduced herself as Mrs. Barry, at once volunteered to help her all she could.

"As far as Baby Faith is concerned," she said, "the child is no trouble to me. I can run in once in a while and see how Mrs. Brixton is getting along, and do the housework."

The Dana girls thanked her for this generous offer. They decided that Mrs. Barry was better-natured than she seemed, although Louise thought that the proposal was based partly on a hope that she might learn something of the widow's affairs. The doctor departed with the assurance that his patient would obey his instructions implicitly, and Jean and Louise decided that it was time for them to return to Starhurst.

Before they left, however, they had a final talk with Mrs. Brixton. Louise was strongly of the opinion that the case should be turned over to the police.

"You see," she explained, "the officers will probably be able to locate this Mr. Tepper, while Jean and I might search for months with no results. After all, we aren't real detectives."

But Mrs. Brixton insisted that the police must not be informed.

"Not for a while, at any rate," she pleaded. "If the police know, then my father will be told. But above all, you mustn't tell my parents about me."

Her anxiety was so great that the Dana girls promised to keep her secret. They felt, however, that these conditions would handicap them a lot in their efforts to locate Miss Tisdale.

"We haven't the faintest idea where to look for this Mr. Tepper," said Louise, as the girls rode back to Starhurst. "I haven't any doubt but that he is responsible for our teacher's disappearance. I suppose he will hold her until he gets his money."

"And in that case," declared Jean shrewdly, "he will probably write to the Tisdales or to Mrs. Brixton. Our best plan is to wait for him to make the first move."

"In fact, it's our only plan. But we should have help."

"Where are we to get help? We can't tell the police."

"Uncle Ned," said Louise with a twinkle in her dark eyes.

Captain Dana, of the transatlantic liner *Balaska,* was the girls' guardian. They were orphans, and since childhood had lived with him and Aunt Harriet, his sister, in Uncle Ned's roomy house on the outskirts of Oak Falls, some little distance from Penfield. Captain Ned had been a second father to the two girls, and they placed great faith in his bluff common sense and his knowledge of the world.

"Perhaps he isn't at home, and if he is, maybe he won't come," objected Jean.

"We'll call the house by long distance and find out," Louise decided.

When they reached Starhurst, they stabled the horses and then put through a telephone call to their home at Oak Falls. To their delight they heard Uncle Ned's voice on the wire.

"Hello! Hello!" he said. "What's all this about? What's wrong?"

"Nothing, Uncle Ned," he was assured. "When did you come home?"

"Yesterday. I'm having a couple of weeks' shore leave. What's the trouble? Run out of money? Left school?"

"Neither," laughed Louise. "But we do want some help."

Then she explained the circumstances surrounding Miss Tisdale's disappearance. Uncle Ned was deeply interested, but he expressed the opinion that they would not need his assistance.

"They'll be hearing from this fellow Tepper before long," he said. "If he demands ransom, it's a case for the police."

"But neither Mrs. Brixton nor Mrs. Tisdale will let us notify the police."

"If they want to see the young woman again, they had better do so," advised Uncle Ned grimly. "That is, unless they want to hand over the ransom and say no more about it."

"There hasn't been any demand for money. That's the puzzling part of it."

"Don't worry. There will be. However, if you think you need me—well, let's say two days from now—let me know and I'll come to Penfield."

The girls were disappointed, yet they realized that their uncle's attitude was sensible and that little could be done until the captors of Miss Tisdale made the next move.

The following day they were surprised and disappointed to find a new instructor of English. Not only was the newcomer austere and unfriendly, but her students soon sensed that they would have to buckle down to extra work.

"Not a bit like Miss Tisdale, is she?" remarked Louise to her sister while they were dressing that afternoon for the final tennis match of the season.

"Certainly isn't," agreed Jean. "But you would have laughed if you had seen the way she squelched Lettie."

"What happened?" asked Louise eagerly.

"Well," explained Jean, "after our class was over, Lettie tried her usual method of making a hit with the new teacher, saying she felt sure she was bound to learn more with her than with anyone else, and wouldn't Miss Cleek have dinner with her soon down in Penfield?"

"But it didn't work, eh?" asked Louise.

"Not for a minute," replied Jean. "Oh, there are the girls," she exclaimed, as the voices of some of their friends were heard urging them, from the ground below their windows, to hurry.

The sisters dashed down the stairs and with their friends soon arrived at the athletic field. In a few moments they were in the midst of a lively set. The Danas were playing doubles against Daisy Martin and Ethel Hoffman in the finals for the autumn cup. Jean was slamming down short, skiddy balls at the net, while Louise's long lobs from behind the back line were very disconcerting to her opponents.

There was wild cheering as the Danas took game after game, and when Daisy and Ethel finally shook hands across the net, admitting defeat and congratulating the sisters, the applause was deafening.

Mrs. Crandall, in awarding the cup, declared she had never seen a finer exhibition of tennis among girls. Louise and Jean modestly accepted the praise, saying they were glad to be able to do it for the honor of Starhurst.

Just then they saw Evelyn Starr running toward them. She came up, panting.

"You're wanted in the office. Telephone call. Very important."

"Who could it be?" asked Louise quickly. "Uncle Ned?"

"I don't think so. You're to call 379 right away. It's a local number."

"Who can it be?" exclaimed Jean, as the girls hastened back to the main building.

They lost no time in calling the number Evelyn had given them. In a moment Louise heard an excited, nervous voice.

"Miss Dana? Oh, I'm so glad. I'm dreadfully upset. Something has happened——"

"Is this Mrs. Brixton?" asked Louise, recognizing the voice.

"Yes. Oh, you must help me. I've received a letter. It came just a few minutes ago and you must—you really *must* get in touch with my mother. The letter is from Amy."

"Is she safe?" asked Louise quickly.

"I imagine so. You were right when you guessed that she is being held for ransom. I'll read you the letter. Listen——"

Mrs. Brixton read the following extraordinary message:

"'DEAR Alice: Please do this. I am not in danger, but tell Mother and also Father that they must be prepared to pay on short notice five thousand dollars. Watch the mail daily for another of these letters. The money is to be paid by Father for my release.'"

"Did the letter come in the mail?" asked Louise.

"Yes. Now I want you to see my mother and tell her to intercept any letters that may come for my father——"

"But Miss Tisdale's message asks you to tell your father that he be prepared to pay the ransom."

"The letter means exactly the opposite of what it says," replied Mrs. Brixton. "You see, it's in code. Amy and I always write to each other in that manner. I suppose the people who are holding her forced her to write that letter to me but she managed to mislead them by using the code. Every fourth word is a word in the real message. What she actually meant by the letter was this: 'Do not tell Father. Be on watch for letters to Father.' The ransom money was in figures so the 'five thousand dollars' counts as one word."

"Then," exclaimed Louise, "she doesn't want your father to pay the money."

"Evidently not. She doesn't want him to know a thing about it, and is afraid a demand for ransom will be sent to him. Perhaps she still thinks she may have a chance of escaping."

"Was the letter postmarked?"

"It was mailed at the Penfield post office. Please don't spend any time trying to trace it just now. I'm afraid the ransom demand may have been mailed to my father at the same time."

"We'll drive out to see your mother at once," Louise promised. "Of course, we won't tell her where we got our information. We'll merely advise her to keep an eye on your father's mail and intercept the ransom letter if it should come.''

''Oh, thank you!'' said Mrs. Brixton warmly. ''But please hurry. There is no time to lose.''

Realizing that the shock of receiving a demand for ransom might have fatal consequences to old Mr. Tisdale, the Dana girls acted promptly. Louise first called Mrs. Tisdale by telephone and warned her to be on the lookout for a ransom letter. Mrs. Tisdale, frightened and bewildered, promised to watch the mail closely.

''But what does it mean?'' she asked. ''Have you had any word from Amy?''

''Jean and I will drive out to see you. We'll explain everything then,'' promised Louise.

The girls went to the garage for Miss Tisdale's coupé and drove immediately to the teacher's home. There, without mentioning Mrs. Brixton or explaining the source of their information, they told the worried woman that her daughter was being held prisoner, but that she was safe and unharmed. They did their best to relieve her of her worries, telling her that they thought Miss Tisdale hoped to escape her captors.

''Otherwise,'' said Jean, ''she wouldn't try to prevent payment of the ransom.''

''If the letter arrives,'' said Mrs. Tisdale, ''I'll see that it doesn't fall into Mr. Tisdale's hands. The shock would be very disastrous.

But what if the messenger calls in person? Or calls him by telephone?"

"We'll have to take a chance on that," said Louise gravely. "And in the meantime Jean and I will do all we can to find out where they have hidden her."

They could stay with Mrs. Tisdale only a few minutes, as they were afraid of being tardy for dinner at Starhurst. On the way back to the school Louise glanced at her wrist watch.

"We'll surely be late."

The speedometer showed thirty-five, then forty miles an hour as the coupé skimmed over the highway. By the time the lights of Starhurst came in view the Penfield city hall clock was chiming the hour of seven.

"Mrs. Crandall will be highly indignant if we're not with the other girls," declared Jean. "We haven't time to take the car into the garage. Leave it in the driveway, and we'll come back for it after dinner."

The coupé skidded to a stop. The girls scrambled out, slammed the door, and raced into the building. They reached the dining hall just in time to take their places.

"Just made it!" Jean gasped gratefully, as she sank into her chair, out of breath.

After dinner, when they sought and received permission to go out and drive the coupé around to the garage, an unpleasant surprise awaited them.

The car was gone!

The Dana girls looked at each other, too stunned for the moment to say a word.

"My goodness!" exclaimed Louise. "It's been stolen."

"But how could it have been stolen?" demanded Jean. "It was locked, wasn't it?"

Louise shook her head mournfully.

"All my fault," she said. "I left the key in the ignition."

They searched the driveway. They even went to the garage, thinking that Zeke Daly might have driven the car in. But the coupé was nowhere to be found.

"There's only one thing to do," said Jean. "We'll have to report it to the police!"

CHAPTER VII

THE CLUE IN THE NOTE

"WE DON'T dare!" exclaimed Louise. "If we tell the police now, they will want to know who owns the car. Then they will ask to question Miss Tisdale. They'll learn she is missing, and the whole story of her strange disappearance will come out."

"I suppose you are right," agreed Jean reluctantly. Then, with a flash of inspiration, she said: "Perhaps the car hasn't been stolen after all. Maybe someone took it as a joke."

"A poor kind of joke," said Louise. "Who would want to do such a thing?"

"It would be just like Lettie Briggs to play a trick like that. Now that I come to think of it, she and Ina Mason left the dining hall early tonight. They looked as if they had something up their sleeves."

"But where would they hide the car?"

"They didn't have more than ten minutes to get away. If they're to blame, they haven't taken the coupé very far. Let's look for it."

"We can't leave the campus without permission, you know."

"Neither could Lettie—if she took the car. So we'll search the grounds first."

As they had no flashlight, they could not look for car tracks on the driveway, but they traveled the length of the winding road around to the garage and stables at the back of the school. They searched at the rear of the brick building, then went out onto the athletic field. They were hoping against hope that the car had not actually been stolen, for they did not relish the prospect of explaining this new disagreeable development to Mrs. Tisdale.

"I can't believe that a car thief would come in off the highway and steal it," said Jean. "Perhaps we ought to wait until daylight to look for it."

"And let Lettie have the laugh on us? I'm going to find that car if I have to stay out here all night."

"But we'll miss study period, and Mrs. Crandall will be angry."

"Come what may," said Louise, "we must locate the coupé."

They went back along the driveway, then explored the grounds beside the road. Finally, beneath the trees about fifty feet from the gravel, the girls saw something big and dark. They advanced toward it in the gloom, and there, safely parked behind some bushes, was the small blue automobile.

Jean breathed a sigh of relief.

"Thank goodness *that* worry is off our minds. I was beginning to think it had been stolen after all."

"Quite a joke," declared Louise grimly. "Come on. We'll take the car back to the garage."

"The worst of it is," said Jean, "we're not sure Lettie was to blame. We can't accuse her of it."

"We'll just have to pretend nothing happened, and by acting that way it will spoil all the fun for her. She probably expects us to come racing into the school, frantic with worry. We'll show her we're not so easily fooled."

They drove the car back into the driveway and then out to the garage. There, under the lights, Louise found a white object on the seat.

"Did you lose your handkerchief?" she asked Jean.

"No. It can't be mine. What heavy perfume! You know I don't drench my handkerchiefs like that."

Louise smoothed out the crumpled bit of linen. Then she chuckled.

"Evidence!"

There was a laundry tag in one corner. It read: "L. Briggs."

Jean laughed with delight.

"Positive proof!" she declared. "Now we know who the guilty one is."

All their resentment over the long search they had been obliged to make for the missing coupé vanished, when they realized that the playful Miss Briggs had convicted herself by leaving the incriminating handkerchief behind.

"She might as well have left her calling card," laughed Louise.

They scrambled out of the coupé, locked the garage and hurried back to the school. Study period had come and gone, and the girls knew that they could not hope to escape a reprimand. That prospect, however, was overshadowed by their delight in knowing that they had turned the tables on Lettie Briggs.

When they went upstairs, they knocked at the door of Lettie's study.

"Come in," said a nasal voice.

As they entered, the Danas found Lettie Briggs and Ina Mason sitting at a table, devouring chocolate candy from a fancy box. Lettie glanced at Ina with a faint smile when she recognized her visitors.

"What is it?" she asked loftily.

"You lost your handkerchief, Lettie," said Louise. "We thought you might be looking for it. We found it on the seat of the car."

Lettie's jaw dropped. The Dana girls almost laughed aloud at her crestfallen and guilty expression.

"Oh—ah—thank you—I didn't know I had lost it—" she stammered.

After gravely giving her the handkerchief, the girls left the room. They fled to their study, unable to restrain their laughter any longer.

The girls spent little time rejoicing in their triumph over Lettie Briggs, for they had a study hour to make up and wanted particularly to be prepared for their English lessons. They were determined that the new instructor should have no cause to find fault with them.

Next day they were glad they had paid special attention to their English lessons. The new teacher, a tall, thin woman, believed in work and plenty of it. In Jean's class she took up the current chapter of *David Copperfield* with the air of one who is determined to stand for no nonsense, and when the lesson was over she assigned so much outside reading that the students gasped.

"We'll take up the tempest scene tomorrow," announced Miss Cleek grimly. "All of it. I want this class to be thoroughly prepared. It is evident that you have been regarding this English course as something of a joke. That attitude must and will be changed."

Jean was resentful. This statement seemed to her to be a reflection upon her beloved Miss Tisdale, who had taught the students to look forward to their English recitations as something highly pleasing and worth-while.

"I'm afraid," said Jean to Louise later, "that this Miss Cleek is going to spoil *David Copperfield* for me. I like that book, but if I'm going to have to study it as closely as she wants us to, I'll begin to dislike it."

"How are we ever going to find time to keep at the mystery?" groaned Louise.

After classes that afternoon the Danas were told that a telephone message awaited them at the office. When they reported to Mrs. Crandall, she informed them that they were to call Mrs. Tisdale, who wished to speak to them.

"She has received the ransom letter!" guessed Jean.

But her surmise was wrong. The teacher's mother had not received any demand for money. The very absence of such a message, in fact, had worried her so much that she had decided to take action.

"I have engaged a detective to look for Amy," she told the girls. "I appreciate your help more than I can say, but I realize that your school work takes up a great deal of your time. I'm nearly distracted with worry. Of course, I haven't told Mr. Tisdale anything as yet. The detective will give all his time to the case, and I hope he'll be able to accomplish something."

"Then you haven't been asked to pay ransom?" asked Louise, incredulous.

"There has been no word at all. I can't understand it."

"Perhaps the detective will be able to find Miss Tisdale. We'll do the best we can, too. We have made a little progress, though not much, but I think we're on the right track."

This news encouraged Mrs. Tisdale considerably. She confessed, however, that she was under a nervous strain. The necessity of keeping the secret from her husband, while she was overpowered with worry, had been a great trial.

"Perhaps we should tell her all we know," said Jean when the girls returned to their study. "The detective may be able to get results more quickly if we turn over our clues to him."

Louise, however, objected to this.

"I think we should not do that without Mrs. Brixton's permission. Of course, we could talk to the detective privately and give him our information in confidence."

"We could do that," agreed Jean. "Yes, I suppose we should see Mrs. Brixton first. After all, it's her secret."

At that moment there was a knock at the study door, and Evelyn Starr looked in.

"The afternoon mail just arrived," she said. "There was a letter for you, so I brought it up with my own mail."

She handed the missive to Jean and went to her own room. The address on the envelope was typewritten. Jean opened it and read the contents, Louise meanwhile looking over her shoulder.

"Please come to see me as soon as you can," the letter read. "I have just received further news." It was signed by Mrs. Brixton.

"More news!" exclaimed Jean. "Perhaps *she* has received the ransom letter."

"There's only one way to find out," declared Louise, scurrying about the room in search of her hat. "We'll drive over to Hilton and call on her."

"But how about my English lesson?" wailed Jean. "If I'm not prepared tomorrow morning, that new teacher will have a few things to say to me."

"Bring the book along with you. We'll read the chapter while we're driving to Hilton."

Jean snatched up her copy of *David Copperfield*, and the two girls hurried downstairs and out to the garage. In a few minutes they were speeding toward Hilton. Louise was at the wheel of the coupé, and as she drove Jean had a chance to read the tempest scene from *David Copperfield*.

The minutes passed quickly as she read a powerful description of the great storm in its devastating course across the South of England. Almost before they realized it, the coupé was bumping its way down the winding road that led into Hilton.

"Brr!" said Jean with a shiver, as she closed the book. "What a squall *that* was! This November wind is only a breeze by comparison."

"Well, Miss Cleek can't say you didn't review the lesson, anyway. You might go over it again tonight."

"I'll dream of hurricanes and storms at sea all night long."

When they got out of the car in front of Lone Tree Cottage, they saw Mrs. Brixton at the door. She was expecting them.

"I knew you would come," said the young widow, hastily ushering them into the cottage. "I've had news. Important news. I received another letter from Amy."

"What does she say?" they asked eagerly.

"The letter itself is very much the same as the other note. But she managed to send another message in the code. Look! I'll show it to you."

Mrs. Brixton produced the letter. It was as follows:

"My dear Alice: Am hoping that the five thousand comes soon. Miles and miles away from my parents and you I am very lonesome in this awful place and I am well aware there is no hope of escape. Danger threatens me if Father doesn't send money. Must close now. I'm not worrying for I know he will."

The girls looked at each other blankly.

"But how can he send the money when he hasn't heard the ransom message?" asked Louise. "He wouldn't know where to send it in any case."

Just then Baby Faith entered the room. She came running over to her mother, her big blue eyes shining and the golden curls bobbing.

"Oh, isn't she cute!" cried both the girls.

In no time at all the little girl had made up to her new friends, and after they had played with her a moment, they took up the subject of Miss Tisdale's note.

"I'm wondering about the code part of the message," said Mrs. Brixton, coming back to the epistle. "It contradicts the rest. Every fourth word counts. Let's read it."

The girls checked off the fourth words of the letter. The code message then read:

" . . . am . . . five . . . miles . . . from . . . you . . . lonesome . . . place . . . well . . . no . . . danger . . . Father . . . must . . . not . . . know . . ."

"Five miles away. She is well and in no danger. And Mr. Tisdale must not know," said Louise reflectively.

Jean sat down beside the window, and gazed out at the road.

"I can't make head nor tail of this affair," she said. "Miss Tisdale is being held for ransom, yet no message demanding any money has been received, and she writes to say that her father mustn't be told. Moreover, she knows he is the only person who could pay such a sum."

"It's a comfort to hear that she's well," sighed Mrs. Brixton. "Perhaps she thinks she has a chance of escaping. Oh, I hope so, I hope so," she added with a little sob, as she twisted her handkerchief into a tight ball.

"I wonder where she is," mused Louise. "A lonely place, about five miles from here——"

She was interrupted by a sharp exclamation from Jean.

"I wonder why that man is watching this place," she cried. "He drove past in a car and now he has backed up. He's looking this way, with the oddest expression on his face."

"Perhaps he's trying to find somebody's house," said Louise, looking toward the road.

Mrs. Brixton went to the window, and as she glanced out, caught a glimpse of a small sedan. The man at the wheel was gazing intently at Lone Tree Cottage. But the moment the widow drew the curtains aside he turned his head away quickly, and stepped on the gas pedal. The car leaped forward.

Mrs. Brixton suddenly put her hand to her head and gasped.

"Catch him! Catch him!" she exclaimed. "Don't let him get away! I—I'm sure it's Mr. Tepper!"

CHAPTER VIII

THE MAP

THE young widow's startled cry electrified the girls.

"Tepper!" exclaimed Louise. "Are you sure?"

"Yes, I'm positive," declared Mrs. Brixton, greatly excited, as she hurried toward the door. "I should recognize that man anywhere."

"We mustn't let him get away!" urged Jean. "We'll follow him."

They ran out, in time to see the car disappearing around the curve at the end of the village street. Louise raced toward the coupé, Jean close at her heels. Hastily they scrambled into the machine. If they could only overtake Mr. Tepper, they felt they might be in a position to clear up the entire mystery of Miss Tisdale's disappearance.

The coupé sped down the road with a roar, reaching the curve in a cloud of dust. Jean, peering through the windshield, caught sight of another car some distance ahead of them.

"There he is!"

Mr. Tepper was wasting no time in hurrying

away from Hilton. He was already more than a quarter of a mile ahead of them, and was steadily increasing his lead. Louise, clinging tightly to the wheel, stepped on the accelerator and drove as rapidly as she dared.

"Perhaps it isn't Mr. Tepper after all," Jean ventured.

"Why should he clear out in such a hurry if he hasn't something on his conscience?" asked Louise. "I think he was planning to call on Mrs. Brixton and ask for the ransom money. When he saw our car in front of the house, he was afraid to come in."

The automobile had disappeared again, this time around a bend in the winding road. Louise was determined to keep the fugitive within sight at all costs. It was possible, she argued, that the man did not know he was being followed.

"In that case," she said, "he may lead us right to the place where Miss Tisdale is hidden."

"I'm afraid we'll have no such luck," said Jean, "but wouldn't it be great if we should?"

They rounded the bend and caught sight of the car again. It was still pulling away from them, for it was a more powerful machine than theirs. Suddenly Jean cried out in excitement:

"Look! He's slowing down! The road is blocked!"

Far ahead they could see a group of workmen engaged in repairing the highway. A small barricade with a red flag had been set up, while beyond this the girls could see a grader in operation.

The fleeing driver pulled up to the obstruction. They saw him alight and begin to argue with the workmen.

"He's trying to talk them into letting him go past!" declared Jean. "Drive, Lou! Drive!"

The coupé skidded wildly on a patch of loose gravel. It veered toward the ditch, and only skillful handling on Louise's part prevented an upset. The auto plunged back onto the road again, however, and went roaring down the half-mile stretch toward the barricade.

By this time the fugitive had evidently persuaded the road crew to let him through, for he climbed back into his car, while two of the workmen began to lift the barrier aside. Louise's heart sank.

"If we can get there in time, they'll let us go through as well," she said.

The other machine drove on, pulling slowly past the grader, and then increased its speed. Swiftly it raced on toward the main highway.

The workmen, seeing the approaching coupé, did not immediately replace the planks that had blocked the road. The man at the wheel of the grader, however, was facing in the other direction, and was gradually swinging his machine out toward the middle of the highway, until at last its huge flanges extended from ditch to ditch.

The girls gasped in dismay.

"Oh, why couldn't he have waited another minute?" demanded Louise in exasperation. "We'll never overtake that car now."

This became obvious when they reached the working crew, brought the coupé to a stop, and found that the man in charge of the grader obstinately refused to pull his machine to the side of the road again.

"If I quit work every time a car comes along," he said, "we'll never finish this job."

"But you let that other auto through," said Jean to the foreman.

"That's different. He was in a hurry. Said he was driving to town for a doctor. You'll just have to wait five or ten minutes until the grader gets up to the highway."

It was fifteen minutes, instead of ten, before this took place. By that time, of course, there was no hope of overtaking the other car. Although they learned it had turned left on the highway, the girls were obliged to give up the chase and drive back to Starhurst. They were disappointed but tried to make the best of the setback.

"Anyway, we don't know for sure that the driver of that car had anything to do with Miss

Tisdale's disappearance,'' said Jean, trying to be cheerful.

"It may not have been Mr. Tepper, after all," added Louise, "although Mrs. Brixton seemed quite certain about it."

That evening, mindful of the extra work the new English teacher had assigned, the girls settled down early to their study period and put all thought of Mr. Tepper out of their minds. For an hour they worked steadily. At last Jean looked up to find Louise poring over a large map of the state. Her English lesson had been thrust aside.

"I thought you were studying your English lesson—not geography," she said.

"I have an idea," said Louise. She picked up a compass and then consulted the scale on which the map was drawn. Setting the little instrument so that it would cover a distance of five miles according to the map, she centered it at Hilton and described a circle.

Jean laughed.

"Think you're going to find the missing Miss Tisdale by driving around the whole thirty-one and three-sevenths miles circumference?"

"Your mental algebra is good tonight!" complimented Louise. She looked at the area enclosed in the circle. "A five-mile radius covers a lot of territory," she murmured.

Jean was interested. She got up and came over to look at the map.

"Miss Tisdale's note said that she was in a deserted place. If we could check off the towns and villages inside the circle—but we need a local map."

"And I know exactly where we can find one," said Louise. "I remember seeing one in Miss Tisdale's study."

"Let's ask Mrs. Crandall for the key."

They hurried out and went downstairs to the Crandall apartment. Mrs. Crandall was out, but Professor Crandall readily gave them the key when they explained their reason for wanting it. The headmistress's husband was a dreamer and extremely good-natured, taking but little part in the life of the school, and asking only that he be let alone. It was rumored that he was writing a book.

"Very strange, this disappearance of Miss Tisdale," he said, shaking his head. "Very perplexing. I cannot imagine what has become of her."

"We have a few clues," said Jean. "Perhaps the map may help us further."

"I hope so," replied Professor Crandall. "Very upsetting to have people drop out of sight like that."

"It's a wonder to me," laughed Jean, when they went back upstairs, "that he even noticed that she was gone."

They went up to the second floor, and followed the corridor to the east wing of the

school. When they came within sight of the
door of Miss Tisdale's study, Louise suddenly
clutched her sister's arm and halted in surprise.

"Why, there's someone in there!" she exclaimed.

Across the corridor floor could be seen a thin
beam of light, which came from beneath the
door.

"Perhaps Miss Tisdale has come back!"
whispered Jean.

"Let's investigate."

Quietly they stole forward. The corridor
was in silence. Louise placed a finger to her
lips and turned.

"Listen!" she whispered.

From beyond the door could be heard the
murmur of voices.

CHAPTER IX

A TALK WITH MR. TISDALE

THE Dana girls listened at the door of Miss Tisdale's study for several minutes. The voices continued. There was a rustling of paper, the sound of a chair being moved across the floor. Two people were in the room, but they spoke so quietly that the girls could not distinguish what they were saying.

"They have no right to be in there, whoever they are," whispered Louise finally. "We have the key. Let's go in."

"Perhaps the door isn't even locked," Jean suggested.

Carefully Louise tried the knob. Finding that the door was not locked, she quickly opened it.

There was a frightened scream. Two figures which had been bending over a desk in the middle of the room suddenly leaped up. The light shone on their startled faces.

"Well," said Louise solemnly, "this *is* a surprise!"

The intruders were none other than Lettie Briggs and Ina Mason!

"What are you doing here?" asked Louise.
Lettie snapped back defiantly:

"What are *you* doing here?"

Louise displayed the key to the study door.
"We got permission from Professor Crandall
to come in here. Did you?"

"Why are you going through Miss Tisdale's
desk?" asked Jean, glancing at the open
drawer.

"We have as much right to solve this mystery as you have," declared Lettie. But her
voice trembled a bit. It was evident that she
was badly frightened.

"Oh, you're trying to solve the mystery?"
said Jean. "But how did you get into this
study without the key? Mrs. Crandall will
want to know how that happened."

"You're not going to tell Mrs. Crandall,
are you?" gasped Ina.

"They wouldn't dare!" snapped Lettie.

"If you do," said Ina, trembling, "you'll
only get us in trouble. We got one of the
chambermaids to leave the door unlocked.
Please don't tell Mrs. Crandall."

Louise shrugged her shoulders. She had no
intention of tattling, but the obvious fear of
the girls somehow amused her.

"We'll see," she said. "You'd better run
along and leave the study to us. We'll lock
up when we go."

The intruders departed hastily. Jean fell

into a chair and laughed until the tears came to her eyes.

"Oh, wasn't that great? Caught in the act! They certainly did look chagrined. I guess they're so frightened they won't be able to sleep a wink tonight."

Louise closed the drawer of the desk.

"Mystery or no mystery, they had no right to go through Miss Tisdale's papers. I suppose they thought they would steal a march on us."

The map she had come to get was hanging on the wall. Louise took it down and rolled it up.

"This is what we want. We'll bring it with us to our own study, and do some close figuring."

They left the room, turning out the lights and carefully locking the door. Back in their own quarters, Louise placed the large map flat on the desk. It contained a layout of the county. Once again Louise took her compass and described a circle to include all the country within a five-mile radius of Hilton.

"Mr. Tepper—if that man *was* Mr. Tepper —turned left on the highway," she said.

"That's so! And look—here's the river! It's inside the circle!" exclaimed Jean excitedly. "That's where we'll look. 'Once a sailor, always a sailor,' " she quoted. "Mr. Tepper was once a sailor. and if he had anything to do with this mystery, he would naturally gravitate toward the river.''

"Your study of *David Copperfield* made you figure that out," laughed Louise. "But you're right, and Tepper was going in that direction when we last saw him in the car."

They consulted the map again. The river wound through a large part of the region within the five-mile circle, and although there were a few villages and towns along its banks, it evidently passed through great stretches of lonely country.

"She may be hidden in any one of a score of places along the water," said Jean.

"Well, Uncle Ned will be here tomorrow, and nobody knows more about navigation than he does."

Jean danced around the room in delight.

"We're on the right track now. I'm sure of it. The mystery is practically solved."

But Louise, more sensible and less impetuous, was not so ready to see victory in sight at this stage of the solution.

"I think," said Jean, "I'll go back to see Mrs. Brixton tomorrow morning. Maybe she'll have some more news. Anyway, I know she is out of money, for she depended entirely upon Miss Tisdale for support. Perhaps I'll get some groceries in town and take them to her."

"That's a good idea," agreed Louise. "And while you're there, why not ask her what she

meant about the note being written on her typewriter? Remember? The note Miss Tisdale
received the day she disappeared.''

"I had forgotten about that. Yes, I'll ask
her. But won't you come, too?''

Louise shook her head.

"I think I'll call on the Tisdales. Perhaps
the ransom message has arrived by now.''

The following morning Jean saddled a horse
from the school stables, and rode off toward
Hilton with a basket of food for the widow.
From various things Mrs. Brixton had said,
Jean surmised that funds in Lone Tree Cottage
were running low, and she knew the groceries
would be appreciated.

As for Louise, she prepared for her visit to
the Tisdales. She had more in mind, however,
than a mere inquiry about the ransom message.
It seemed unnatural to her that Mr. Tisdale
should be so violent in his insistence that Mrs.
Brixton's name never should be mentioned in
his presence.

"After all," she said to herself, "he hasn't
seen his daughter for several years. He is an
old man and knows he may die suddenly any
time. I can hardly believe that he is still vindictive.''

Her plan was to speak to Mr. Tisdale and
learn, if possible, if he was as stubborn in his
attitude as Mrs. Tisdale and the others believed him to be.

Louise

As Jean was ready to go out, she encountered Dr. Malcolm in the hall. He was a fat, jovial physician from Penfield, who officiated as the school doctor. Today he was on his regular weekly visit of inspection.

"Hello, Miss Dana!" he greeted cheerfully. "Need any pills or medicines today? You don't look as if you do."

"None today, thank you, Doctor," laughed Louise. "But I do need some advice."

A sudden thought had occurred to her when she had spied the man of medicine.

"Advice?" asked Dr. Malcolm. "What is it? Not thinking of going on a diet, are you? You're not overweight."

"No, it has nothing to do with me. Doctor, if a person is told to avoid sudden shocks, would it be risky to tell him something surprising?"

"Depends on the size of the shock."

"Well, a pleasant shock."

The doctor laughed.

"I've heard of people 'dying of joy,' but not often," he said. "Most people have pretty good constitutions when it comes to hearing pleasant news—or bad news either, for that matter. If they are greatly frightened, it's another matter. If you have any surprising news to break to a person in that condition, just lead up to it gradually and it won't kill him."

Louise weighed the physician's words as she drove out to the Tisdale place that morning. If she could contrive some way of learning the father's real feelings toward Mrs. Brixton, without actually bringing the widow's name into the conversation, she felt that she could make progress.

"If he knew she was in trouble and that she needed him, I daresay he'd help her," thought Louise. "He seems a very crochety old man, but I think his bark is worse than his bite."

Mr. Tisdale, contrary to her expectations, was in remarkably good spirits when she called at tne Tisdale home. He was sitting out in the garden, despite the fact that the weather was cold, and the sunshine not very strong.

"Sunshine and fresh air!" exclaimed the old gentleman. "Best medicine in the world. It's what keeps me alive."

"I think you're looking much better, Mr. Tisdale," said Louise, thinking this would cheer him up. However, he did not seem at all pleased to hear this.

"You think so?" he asked sharply. "Well, it just shows that you can't go by looks. I'm not well at all. Didn't sleep a wink last night. My back hurts me. If it wasn't for getting out in the sunshine once in a while, I'd be in my grave. Sit down and talk to me. Not many people come to see me nowadays. Can't be bothered talking to an old fellow with one foot in the grave. Even my own daughter won't come to see me. Amy didn't come last week-end.''

"Perhaps she couldn't get away," said Louise uneasily.

"That's what her mother said. Oh, well," sighed Mr. Tisdale heavily, "when you're old and gray and useless, you can't expect any consideration from your own children."

"I don't agree with you there, Mr. Tisdale," replied Louise. "Even if I did, I think that parents are inclined to forgive their children almost anything. If you had a son, for in-stance, and he ran away——"

"What's that?" barked the old man fiercely. "A son? I haven't a son."

"But *if* you had. And if he ran away and treated you very bad——"

"I'd disown him. I'd cut him off without a cent."

"Perhaps. But if you learned that he was in dreadful trouble and that he needed your help, I really think you'd do all you could to aid him."

"I would, eh?" snapped Mr. Tisdale. "Well —I don't know." He became thoughtful. "Maybe. It's hard to say. Maybe I would. But I haven't a son and he hasn't run away and he isn't in trouble, so what's the sense of talking about it?"

Louise could get no more out of him than

that, but it was sufficient to encourage her in the belief that Mr. Tisdale's bad nature, like his ill health, was not quite as hopeless as he would like people to believe.

Mrs. Tisdale was not at home. The old gentleman explained that she had gone to Penfield on business. He complained that she seemed to have a great deal on her mind, and that she failed to confide in him any more.

"But that's the way of the world," he groaned. "When you get old, you get put on the shelf, and nobody thinks you're any use to anyone. I suppose I must put up with it."

However, when he said goodbye to Louise a few minutes later, he was especially eager in urging her to give his love to Amy Tisdale.

"Tell her to come out and see me whenever she can. She's the only daughter I have left, and she won't have her poor old father much longer, I'm thinking. I'm liable to drop off any minute."

As Louise drove back to Starhurst, she definitely decided to talk again to this eccentric old man. She was certain he could be won over, and that his help would be invaluable.

Then her thoughts turned to other angles of the mystery. Would Jean have any news? How soon would Uncle Ned arrive? And what would they find when they journeyed to the river?

CHAPTER X

ON THE RIVER

CAPTAIN NED DANA, uncle and guardian of the girls, was deeply attached to his two lively young nieces. Their plea to him for help in solving the mystery had amused him, but nevertheless he took the trouble to journey to Starhurst. More than that, he had telephoned Mrs. Crandall on the previous evening and asked that the girls be allowed the day off.

The hardy, good-natured skipper of the *Balaska* arrived at the school after luncheon. For a full half hour after his enthusiastic welcome by the girls he listened to an excited and more or less incoherent account of the events surrounding Miss Tisdale's disappearance.

"Well," he said finally, "I can't quite make head nor tail of it yet. But you figure there's a sailor mixed up in the mystery, and that your teacher is hidden somewhere along the river. Maybe I'd better go with you in the car and talk to Mrs. Brixton. With both of you chattering at once, I'm getting tangled up more and more every minute."

"It was good of you to come, Uncle Ned!"

exclaimed Jean, as they got into the car. "We have lots and lots of clues, you see, but we don't know yet how to fit them together."

Uncle Ned laughed.

"From your letters," he said, "your Aunt Harriet and I almost thought you had come to a school for detectives instead of a young ladies' seminary!"

"Oh, we don't neglect our school work," Louise assured him. "But when there's a mystery——"

"You just can't resist it, eh? Well, of course, when you're good at solving mysteries I don't blame you a bit. After all, you cleared up that affair of the study lamp all right. Now, let me get this straight. Your teacher was working to support her sister, who ran away and married a fellow named Brixton, and this Brixton had a partner named Tepper."

"Who was a sailor," added Jean.

"And this Mr. Tepper was seen talking to your teacher before she disappeared. There hasn't been any demand for ransom. That's the queer part of it."

As Louise drove the car toward Hilton she explained the circumstances of Mr. Tisdale's illness and his resentment toward Mrs. Brixton.

"That makes it even harder," said Uncle Ned. "If he wasn't a sick man I'd just go to him and I'd say, 'Look here. One of your daughters is missing and the other is nearly starving to death, so you'd better get busy and do something about it.' However, if the shock is likely to kill him, we'd better be careful."

"I really think he would do everything he could to help," admitted Louise. "But we can't afford to take any chances."

"We'll see what Mrs. Brixton thinks about it. Maybe she can tell us a few things about this man Tepper."

However, when they reached Hilton and knocked at the entrance to Lone Tree Cottage, no one answered. Louise tried to open the door, but it was locked.

"That's funny," grumbled Uncle Ned. "I thought you said she wasn't well."

"She was sick in bed when I called on her this morning," said Jean. "I came to look at her typewriter and compare the writing with that in the note that was sent to Miss Tisdale."

"What did you learn?" asked Louise.

"That the note was written on a typewriter just like it, but that it wasn't the same machine."

Uncle Ned thrust his hat to the back of his head and gazed ruefully at the locked door.

"Guess we're on a wild-goose chase," he said. "It seems strange to me that a woman can be sick in bed one minute and away the next. Do you think she's entirely trustworthy?"

"Oh, we're sure of it!" exclaimed Louise.

No suspicion of Mrs. Brixton's good faith had ever crossed their minds.

"In an affair like this," commented Uncle Ned, "you can't trust anybody. She and this sailor may be in league."

"I can't see how that could be possible," declared Jean. "Why should she be mixed up in the disappearance of her own sister?"

"Are you *sure* she is Miss Tisdale's sister? What proof have you of that?"

"We have her word for it," suggested Jean.

Their uncle shook his head.

"That's what she told you when you came here looking for information. And she wouldn't let you tell Mr. and Mrs. Tisdale anything about her, eh? Well now, if I were you, I'd just move along sort of careful. You can't tell what you may be getting into."

"Baby Faith is darling," said Louise. "Surely her mother couldn't be a crook!" she added.

The Dana girls were not at all convinced that their uncle was on the right track. Nevertheless, they did agree that they knew very little about Mrs. Brixton. Was it possible, they began to ask themselves, that she was actually associated with Tepper and had been misleading them from the beginning?

"No use staying here any longer," said Uncle Ned. "Let's look for that river you were telling me about."

"He was heading toward the river when we last saw him," said Jean.

As they drove back toward the main highway and then turned in the direction of the water, as shown on their map, the girls were silent. They did not put much faith in Uncle Ned's theory that Mrs. Brixton might not be trustworthy, yet the possibility opened up many new lines of thought. Privately, they resolved to be wary in their dealings with the young widow until they were convinced that her identity was definitely established. Some of the neighbor woman's scornful remarks recurred to them, adding new fuel to their doubts.

The highway dipped suddenly, and they could see the winding course of the river below. There was a bridge across the stream, and a small settlement of about a dozen houses and a general store nestled on the banks.

"Let's stop off here and have some hot chocolate," suggested Louise. "Maybe we'll learn something."

A few idlers looked at them curiously as they entered the store. Uncle Ned ordered three bottles of ginger ale, as that was all the place could boast of in the way of liquid refreshment. Many years at sea had made Captain Dana a master of the art of striking up conversations, and within a few minutes he was talking freely with the men who stood about.

He did not make the mistake of appearing

to be inquisitive, yet he gradually led up to a casual inquiry as to whether any strangers had recently moved into the neighborhood. It appeared that there had been none, "except on the river."

"I suppose there's a good bit of traffic there now," said Uncle Ned, sipping his ginger ale.

"It ain't like it used to be," said one of the men. "Of course, there's boats comin' and goin' all the time, but not many. It's gettin' late in the year anyway."

"I was hoping we'd be able to take a little boat ride," mused Captain Dana.

"Lem Wilkes has a motor boat that he rents out by the hour," volunteered the storekeeper.

"That's fine. What do you say, girls? Care to come for a little spin?"

The girls eagerly agreed, and they set out in search of Lem Wilkes, whom they eventually located in his boathouse a few hundred yards below the bridge. Mr. Wilkes was a melancholy, angular man who seemed greatly surprised at any request for his craft at this time of year.

"Looks like snow," he grumbled. "Never heard of folks goin' joy-ridin' on the river in November. It's your affair, though. I was just thinkin' of bringin' the boat in today and puttin' her away for the winter."

The craft was a heavy, clumsy-looking affair, reeking of oil and fish scales. Mr. Wilkes mournfully observed that he would lend them a tin can "in case she springs a leak," filled up the gasoline tank, and then spent ten minutes heroically laboring to start the engine. For a while it looked as if the boat ride would not materialize, but finally the engine responded with a roar and a dense cloud of black fumes. The girls climbed in, while Uncle Ned took his place at the wheel. Soon they were heading slowly out into midstream.

"What a scow!" growled Uncle Ned in disgust.

"Not much like the *Balaska,* is it?" laughed Jean.

"It's a good thing my first mate can't see me now. If he ever spied me at the wheel of a tub like this, he'd laugh himself sick. Why did we come out here, anyway?"

The late November afternoon was cold and cloudy. The river was swept by a stiff breeze, and although the girls had worn warm coats, they were soon chilled by the biting wind that cut across the water.

"Now," repeated Uncle Ned, "what are we looking for?"

"Miss Tisdale," replied Jean.

"Well, Jean, keep your eyes open," laughed Uncle Ned. "Watch those trees along the shore. She may be hiding behind one of them."

The girls smiled at Uncle Ned's droll humor, but they had their own ideas. When they left the little settlement behind and came to a section of the river bordered by lonely farmlands, they kept a sharp lookout for any abandoned houses that might serve as possible hiding places.

After half an hour Uncle Ned announced that he was resigning as captain.

"We're going to make port!" he said, bringing the cumbersome launch around. "There's a storm brewing."

As the boat headed north again the girls saw that heavy clouds had gathered. The craft was now plunging directly into waves that were growing more choppy every instant. The wind became more intense and the temperature dropped. The girls huddled together for warmth against the stinging gale.

In a few minutes they noticed a gray mist hanging over the surface of the river. Whipped by the strong north blasts, a blinding snow flurry began to sweep down upon them. The boat pitched and tossed. Uncle Ned kept a firm hand on the wheel, and his eyes narrowed as he peered ahead through the swirling flakes.

Weakened by the buffeting of the waves, and drenched with water as great billows broke over the bow, the launch began to leak. Jean and Louise were forced to take turns bailing out water with the tin can. The snowstorm swept down with such violence and fury that it seemed as if the old boat must surely capsize.

Within a few minutes the entire surface of the river was in a blinding turmoil of slashing snow and leaping waves, completely hiding the shore from view.

"Hold tight!" roared Uncle Ned. "I've been in worse squalls than this, so we'll get out of this one. But hold tight!"

The girls knew that they were safe with Uncle Ned at the helm, but that was only small consolation when they were drenched and shivering. They clung desperately to the sides of the pitching craft, bailing out water incessantly, and heartily wishing they had never thought of exploring the river.

The storm was so wild that they could scarcely see more than a few yards ahead, when suddenly, above the howling of the wind, they heard a heavy, throbbing sound. It was the roar of a powerful motor.

"Another boat!" cried Louise.

Even as Jean spoke, they saw a dark shadow loom up out of the white mist immediately ahead of them. A big launch, riding at terrific speed, came hurtling out of the storm.

"Look out!" shouted Uncle Ned. "You're going to run us down!"

The wind hurled the shout back into his teeth. The oncoming craft did not alter its course by an inch. With motor wide open it bore down swiftly upon the defenseless little launch!

CHAPTER XI

A Narrow Escape

The swift and sudden approach of the other boat had not disconcerted Captain Dana and the girls at first, because they assumed that the craft would alter its course to pass them. When they saw the sharp bow of the speedboat slicing the waves only a few yards away and coming directly toward them, they awoke to a quick realization of their peril. The pilot had evidently not seen them in the storm. And now their launch lay directly in his course.

Jean covered her eyes to shut out the sight of the oncoming speedboat, while Louise gritted her teeth and held her breath. Uncle Ned shouted and bore down on the wheel.

The cumbersome old launch was slow to respond. It swung sluggishly to the left.

The Captain's rugged face was stern. In an instant he had calculated every detail—the intervening distance, the speed of the other boat, their own speed, and the retarding force of wind and waves. He realized that they had one slight chance, and let out another stentorian roar of warning as he swung the wheel over hard and tried to pull the launch out of danger.

It was all over in a few seconds. The speed-boat was upon them just as the rudder re-sponded to Captain Dana's expert handling of the wheel. It swept past the stern of the little launch with inches to spare. In the next mo-ment the Dana craft was rocking wildly on the crest of the other's heavy swell. Uncle Ned quickly turned the wheel again, this time to put them head-on to the speedboat's wake.

They lurched wildly. Water poured over the side, as a great wave broke upon them. The boat rose and dipped, as the mysterious speed-boat vanished into the snowy mist that over-hung the river.

"If he'd run us down we'd have been drowned sure!" he declared. "We shouldn't have lasted three minutes in that icy water."

The girls were shaken by their narrow es-cape, but Uncle Ned stuttered with rage.

"It was Tepper!" cried Louise, when she had recovered her breath.

"What's that?" shouted Uncle Ned. "Tep-per? Do you mean it?"

"I saw his face distinctly as he went by. I'm sure the man was Mr. Tepper. He wasn't more than three feet away. He was at the wheel." Louise was greatly excited. "Let's follow him, Uncle Ned."

"I'd like to," he said. "Nothing would suit me better than to lay my hands on that fellow and teach him something about rules for pilots. But his boat's too fast for us. We'd never catch him, and in this storm we couldn't even get a glimpse of him.''

They realized that he was right. It was disappointing to think that they had been so close to Sailor Tepper and yet were powerless to overtake him.

''You're sure the man was Tepper?'' asked Uncle Ned.

''It was the man I saw in the car outside Lone Tree Cottage,'' replied Jean. ''I should recognize him anywhere.''

''Perhaps he tried to run us down on purpose,'' said Louise.

''I don't believe so,'' came from Uncle Ned promptly. ''He would have wrecked his own boat doing that. No, he was just in an awful hurry to get somewhere and he came pounding out of that storm with his head down and never even saw us.''

''Well,'' said Jean, ''it's lucky we saw *him,* anyway.''

''I'll meet that fellow yet and tell him what's what,'' promised Uncle Ned grimly. ''In the meantime, I think we'd better be getting back to Starhurst. You girls will be catching your death of cold if you don't get a change of clothing soon.''

The launch headed up the river again, and into the storm. By the time the trio reached the boathouse about ten minutes later, the girls were "frozen stiff," as Jean expressed it. They found Lem Wilkes waiting for them. He was evidently greatly surprised to see them all.

"Beginnin' to think I'd never see my boat again," he told them. "Thought you'd be swamped sure."

"We came close to it," said Uncle Ned. "A speedboat nearly ran us down."

"Speedboat, eh?" said the boatman. "I heard it go past. Didn't see it, though. It was out in the middle of the river and the storm was too heavy."

"Do you know anyone who runs a speedboat on the river?"

"I know *that* boat. Reckernize the sound of its engine," said Lem Wilkes. "It's been runnin' up and down here quite a lot this past week."

"Where's its home port?" demanded Uncle Ned, interestedly.

The boatman had no information about the mysterious craft. He did not know who owned it and could give only a sketchy description of its appearance. Questioned further by Uncle Ned, he said he had never heard of anyone on the river who answered to the name of Tepper.

"Don't put your boat away for the winter just yet," said Uncle Ned, as he paid the man for the use of the launch. "We may want to use it again."

Lem Wilkes promised that the craft would be available whenever they might want it. He also said he would not fail to caulk up the seams and make it more seaworthy.

"If you can find out anything about that speedboat," called Jean, as they were leaving, "please make a note of it for us."

Louise drove back to Starhurst in record time, and the Dana girls hastened to their rooms where they changed into dry clothing. Mrs. Crandall had invited Uncle Ned to have dinner at the school, and when Jean and Louise went downstairs, they found him in the center of a group of admiring girls. He was telling sea stories, and was in the middle of a tale about a voyage he had taken many years before as first mate of a steamer along the cost of Africa.

"Oh, Captain Dana," gushed Lettie Briggs, showing her prominent front teeth in a smile that was meant to be ingratiating, "I think you're just too wonderful! Won't you sit beside me at dinner? I'd like to hear more of your adventures."

"I'm sorry," replied Uncle Ned, "but I've arranged to sit with my nieces. One on each side of me."

Lettie Briggs looked discomfited. It was evident that she had expected Uncle Ned to show some appreciation of the honor she thought she was conferring upon him.

The evening meal was a great success, for Uncle Ned was in rare form and told story after story. He had experienced countless adventures in odd corners of the world, and his mariner's slang added a piquant touch to his tales. The girls were unanimous in declaring him to be the most interesting visitor Starhurst had entertained in many a day.

After dinner he went up to the study with Jean and Louise, where they discussed for some time various phases of the mystery of Miss Tisdale's disappearance. Uncle Ned concurred in the opinion of the girls that they had made decided progress in discovering that Tepper was actually frequenting the river.

"Let's go back there tomorrow," suggested Louise. "If we can find that speedboat, we'll find Tepper."

"And if I lay my hands on him," said Uncle Ned, "he'll have some explaining to do."

"I wish Mrs. Crandall would give us another holiday," put in Jean.

"Hold on! Hold on!" laughed Uncle Ned. "Did you come to school to study or to solve mysteries? No indeed! You attend classes tomorrow, and after school's out, we'll drive over to the river."

"If you are going back to Oak Falls the day after tomorrow, we'll scarcely have any time to work on the mystery with you."

"Can't help it," said Uncle Ned. "Perhaps

we can locate that speedboat tomorrow after noon, and then it won't take us long to find out something.'' With that they had to be content.

Next day it seemed as if classes would never end. As soon as the three o'clock gong sounded, the Dana girls made a wild rush to their rooms. Hurriedly they changed into their warmest clothing. Although there had been no more snow, they knew that it would be cold out on the water.

Uncle Ned was waiting for them, and they lost ro time in getting the car out of the garage, for they realized that they would have only a short time on the river before darkness should fall. When they reached the settlement at the bridge, they found to their delight that Lem Wilkes was in his boathouse and that the launch was ready for them. He had, as he had promised, caulked up the seams and had also effected a few repairs to the engine so that it started without delay.

"Away we go, then!" said Uncle Ned. "Let's get on the trail of that speedboat."

They traveled down the river for several miles but could find no boathouses. In none of the little bays that might have sheltered the craft did they see any sign of the one for which they were looking.

"Maybe we're going the wrong way," suggested Jean.

"His home port may be up the river instead of down," agreed Uncle Ned. "We'll go back and take a look around."

Twilight was not far off when they again passed the settlement on their return journey.

"We have wasted our time," said Louise. "It will be dark before we go much farther, I'm afraid."

"Let's stay as long as the light holds out," suggested Jean.

The upper reaches of the river were lonely, with heavily wooded shores and many small bays, which at last gave way to a desolate, marshy stretch where great areas of weeds extended far out into the water.

"Have to stay in the middle of the river or we're apt to run aground," Uncle Ned remarked. "The water is shallow along these shores."

A channel had been marked out by stakes that protruded above the surface. Captain Dana held the launch in mid-channel. With twilight descending it was difficult to study the shoreline.

"Guess we'd better turn back," he said at last. "It's too dark to see anything."

"Just a minute!" Louise exclaimed suddenly. "What's that among the weeds, over to the left?"

Uncle Ned brought the launch a few hundred yards upstream. Out among the grasses they could see a sleek, dark craft tied to an anchored float.

"It's the speedboat!" declared Jean in excitement.

Uncle Ned studied the object carefully.

"It's *a* speedboat," he said, "but maybe it isn't the one we're after."

"It looks just like the boat that almost ran us down yesterday," Louise contended.

"I wish we could get closer to it. But the water is too shallow. We'll go aground if we run out of the channel," said Uncle Ned.

"And it's much too cold for a swim," said Jean disconsolately. "Just our luck!"

"If that's Tepper's boat, then where is he?" asked Louise, puzzled. "He must have gone ashore in a rowboat."

They were balked again. Darkness was coming on, and much as they hated to leave the spot, they had to turn about and go back down the river. They believed they had found Tepper's boat, but the man himself was as far from reach as ever.

CHAPTER XII

Two Visits

"UNCLE NED," said Jean, on the way back to Starhurst, "we *must* have the day off tomorrow. It's only once in a blue moon that you come to Starhurst."

"Depends on what Mrs. Crandall says," answered Captain Dana noncommittally.

"Please ask her," begged Louise.

"Oho! You want *me* to do the asking. You're afraid she'll turn you down," he laughed.

"Well, she might."

The girls knew that it was extremely probable that the request would be refused if they were to make it themselves.

"Well, it's true I haven't seen much of you on this visit," said their uncle. "Maybe your headmistress will not like the idea—but I'll ask her, anyway. Yet if your marks show up poorly at Christmas time, she'll blame me."

Uncle Ned had to use considerable tact and diplomacy to convince Mrs. Crandall that the Dana girls should be granted the holiday. She raised many objections, making the tart comment that they seemed more interested in mysteries than in their studies. Finally, however, she granted them permission to stay away from classes the following day. The girls were jubilant.

"Now we'll get somewhere," declared Jean. "Uncle Ned has helped us a great deal so far. We'll take him out to the Tisdales. I'd like to know if Mrs. Tisdale has had any report from her detective."

"And then we'll go back and see Mrs. Brixton."

"Do you believe she is the *real* Mrs. Brixton?"

"I don't know what to think. If she is deceiving us, she is a good actress," said Louise.

Shortly after nine o'clock the next morning they all set out for the home of their teacher. Louise had thoughtfully brought along a book as a present for Mr. Tisdale as an excuse for calling.

"I'll talk to the old gentleman," said Uncle Ned, as they made their plans. "That will give you two a chance to have a chat with Mrs. Tisdale. She hasn't seen this woman who calls herself Mrs. Brixton, has she?"

"We haven't said a word about her."

"Do you think that's wise? It seems to me she ought to know that much, anyway. If you can bring the two of them face to face, so much the better. If this Mrs. Brixton is really her daughter, Mrs. Tisdale will be able to help her, even without telling her husband.''

The girls agreed that this was sensible advice. When they reached their destination, old Mr. Tisdale was introduced to Uncle Ned. So great was the captain's ability for making friends that within a short time the two men were chatting as if they had known each other for years. Captain Dana won Mr. Tisdale's heart at once by sympathizing with him in his illnesses and by inviting him to describe his various ailments. He then volunteered an account of an operation he had once undergone. Mr. Tisdale, highly delighted, came back with the story of *his* operation. Uncle Ned then offered an account of a siege of rheumatism, and Mr. Tisdale traded an attack of asthma for it, both at considerable length. Within ten minutes it was obvious that Mr. Tisdale regarded the sea captain as the most interesting and sympathetic man he had ever met.

The girls slipped away and went into the house where they seized an opportunity to have an uninterrupted talk with Mrs. Tisdale.

''Have you had any word from your detective yet?'' they asked eagerly.

Mrs. Tisdale shook her head. It was evident that the strain of her daughter's disappearance was telling on her, for she looked pale and worried.

''I have heard from him,'' she said, ''but he

has made very little, if any, progress. Time and again I've been tempted to tell my husband everything and call in the police. For all I know, my poor child may have been slain.''

The girls hastened to put her fears at rest. They had decided to tell her about Mrs. Brixton and this seemed to be the proper time.

"Miss Tisdale is quite safe," announced Louise.

"What do you mean? I don't understand. How do you know?"

"We have seen a message from her. She is being held in a lonely place several miles from Penfield, but has come to no harm."

"A message?" exclaimed Mrs. Tisdale. "Oh, please let me see it. How did she manage to send word to you?"

She was greatly excited. This was only natural, for it was the first definite news of Miss Tisdale since the teacher had disappeared.

"The letter wasn't sent to us," Jean said. "It was sent to Mrs. Brixton."

Mrs. Tisdale gazed at them in complete bewilderment.

"Mrs. Brixton!" she exclaimed. "You don't mean—you can't mean—Alice!" Mrs. Tisdale's face blanched, and for a moment she looked as if she were going to faint.

Quickly the girls explained how they had located Mrs. Brixton and Baby Faith in Hilton.

They related how Miss Tisdale had been supporting her widowed sister, and how she had concealed the fact because she feared her father's anger. They explained that Mrs. Brixton had asked them to keep the secret of Lone Tree Cottage, but that they now felt no good would be gained by withholding the facts any longer.

"Naturally," said Louise, "we haven't told Mr. Tisdale anything of this. But we thought that you should know."

Mrs. Tisdale's gentle face was a study in amazement and incredulity. She could scarcely speak, so great was her surprise. Finally she stammered:

"Why—my dears—it has been my greatest wish to learn where Alice is living—I—I don't know how to thank you——"

Emotion overcame her. She burst into tears of joy and relief. After a while she looked up.

"To think she has been living so close to me all this time," she said, "and I didn't know it. You'll take me to see her, won't you? Of course, I dare not let Mr. Tisdale know just yet—I'm afraid he is still very angry with Alice —but if I could go alone I might be able to help her."

The girls promised to drive Mrs. Tisdale to Hilton as soon as possible. They realized that it was difficult for her to leave the house even for a short while without arousing her husband's suspicions, but she said she would contrive to have some sort of an excuse for an afternoon's absence later in the week.

"You have done so well," she said gratefully, "that I wish you would coöperate with the detective I engaged. After all, he has more time to spend on the case, while you have your school duties. Will you do that for me?"

They promised to assist the man in any way they possibly could. The conversation was cut short just then, because Mr. Tisdale hobbled into the room, followed by Uncle Ned. The elderly invalid was obviously on such good terms with Captain Dana that he extended a general invitation to all of them to remain to luncheon.

"Can't eat very much myself," he said. "A man in my poor health must watch his diet. But if you'll take potluck with us, you're more than welcome."

Uncle Ned glanced at his watch.

"I'm to catch the three-fifteen train," he said, "and we have another call to make——"

"No excuses. No excuses, Captain Dana!" said Mr. Tisdale brusquely. "You must stay to eat. I want to tell you about a very interesting case—happened to a friend of mine—name of Higgins. It seemed he had been suffering from throat trouble for several years——"

He was off into a dreary medical anecdote.

When he had explained the circumstances of the unfortunate Higgins's trouble and its eventual cure, he launched into another lengthy tale in which all the characters were suffering from various serious ailments. Mr. Tisdale was enjoying himself immensely, and kept up his flow of conversation throughout luncheon. His guests were obliged to listen, although they became extremely bored finally.

When Captain Dana and the girls took their departure shortly after one o'clock, it was with a cordial invitation to come again. Mr. Tisdale, having been permitted to talk about diseases to his heart's content, looked more cheerful than he had in a long time.

"Never saw such a man!" grumbled Uncle Ned, as they drove away. "I guess he's ill, all right, but he isn't half as bad as he thinks he is."

They passed through Penfield and on out to Hilton. En route Uncle Ned expressed the belief that Mr. Tisdale's fear of a sudden shock was "all bosh." He did not believe it would harm him to learn about Mrs. Brixton.

"That is," he said cautiously, "if this woman *is* Mrs. Brixton."

When they reached Lone Tree Cottage they found, to their relief, that the young widow was again at home. After one glance at her pale, careworn face, the Dana girls forgot any doubt they might have had as to her identity.

Her graciousness and sweet dignity in this time of anxiety restored the faith of Jean and Louise in her.

As for Uncle Ned, who was very fond of children, he seemed to lose all his misgivings the moment he spied Baby Faith. He picked the lovely child up in his arms, put her on his knee, and even recited jingles to her.

When Jean and Louise told Mrs. Brixton of the progress they had made on the mystery and of their encounter with Tepper in the speedboat, she became very tense. Uncle Ned took a vigorous part in the discussion, questioning Mrs. Brixton closely on many details of her past life and of the history of Sailor Tepper. Apparently he was well satisfied with her replies, and was no longer suspicious that she might be playing a part.

"This is a queer business," said Captain Dana gravely, "and I don't really know what to think of it. There should be a ransom message by now. But there isn't. I'd like to find out about this fellow Tepper. Maybe your husband owed him five thousand dollars. Maybe not. But I'll look up the business affairs of the firm of Brixton and Tepper, and perhaps I'll get some information."

Mrs. Brixton thanked him warmly for his help, but he waved aside her protestations of gratitude.

"No trouble at all. I have another week's

shore leave. A great many things can happen in that time.''

Suddenly he looked at his watch.

''Half-past two!'' exclaimed Uncle Ned. ''And my train leaves at three-fifteen! Where's my hat?''

The girls left hurriedly with their guardian, but Louise found time to draw Mrs. Brixton to one side and press a twenty-dollar bill into her hand.

''From your mother,'' she whispered. ''She asked me to give it to you. And she's coming to see you as soon as she can.''

''Then you told her?'' gasped the excited young woman.

''Yes. And I'm glad we did. She was so overjoyed——''

''Hurry!'' bellowed Uncle Ned from the doorway. ''I'll miss that train.''

''How can I thank you?'' exclaimed the widow. ''This money is very welcome. I've been so distracted with worry that I could scarcely sleep. You don't know how grateful I am for your help——''

''Don't thank me,'' laughed Louise. ''Thank your mother—when she comes to see you.''

She ran out of the house with Jean and joined Uncle Ned, who was waiting impatiently beside the car. They were soon speeding toward Penfield, where Captain Dana dashed into his hotel, packed, checked out, and scrambled back into the waiting auto. They reached the station just in time to see the train pulling in. Calling a hasty farewell and a promise to write, Uncle Ned hastened across the platform and climbed aboard.

"And that," said Jean, as they drove back to Starhurst, "ends the excitement for today."

But she was wrong. When they returned to the school they were met by one of the maids, who informed them that a stranger was waiting to see them in the library.

CHAPTER XIII

THE HOUSE NEAR THE RIVER

"A MAN?" asked Jean.

"Yes, Miss Dana," replied the maid. "He arrived a few minutes ago. I knew you would be back after you saw your uncle off on the train, so I asked him to wait."

"My hair is so untidy!" said Louise. "You talk to him, Jean, while I run upstairs and fix up."

She hurried off to the study. Jean, who was not so particular about appearances, sauntered into the library. A stout, sandy-haired man with a red face was sitting in a corner, balancing his hat on one knee and looking as if he would rather be anywhere else than in a girls' school.

"Miss Dana?" he asked.

"Yes. I am Jean Dana."

"My name's Boltwood," said the sandy-haired man. "Mrs. Tisdale was speaking to me over the phone and she said I ought to drop around and see you and your sister. I'm a detective, and she tells me we're—well—working on the same case."

119

"I'm very glad to meet you, Mr. Boltwood," said Jean, suddenly excited by the realization that this was the real flesh-and-blood detective engaged by Mrs. Tisdale. "Do you mind waiting a few minutes longer? My sister will be down in a little while. I'll go and tell her you are here."

She scurried out of the library. Mr. Boltwood, looking somewhat astonished, heaved a sigh, sat down again and resumed his occupation of balancing his hat on his knee.

As Jean ran upstairs to inform Louise as to the identity of their visitor, she met Lettie Briggs on the landing.

"Hello," drawled Lettie. "I hear you had the day off. It's nice to be some people. Mrs. Crandall must be thinking of adopting you."

Into Jean's mind flashed an impish thought.

"I'm glad I met you, Lettie," she said. "There's a man in the library—he's been waiting there for the past ten minutes. Didn't someone tell you?"

"Waiting for *me!*" exclaimed Lettie. "A man to see me?"

Lettie was interested, curious, flattered. Inwardly she was wildly excited. She did not even thank Jean for the supposed message, but clattered down the stairs as quickly as her high heels would permit.

If she had looked around, she would have seen that Jean was quietly following her. On

Jean's face was a smile of delicious anticipation.

Lettie Briggs gave her hair a pat, smoothed her skirt and sailed into the library. Mr. Boltwood, who assumed that this angular damsel was the other Dana sister, rose from his chair and bowed.

"How do you do?" he said.

"How do you do?" chirped Lettie in a voice that trembled with excitement. It was seldom that anyone called at Starhurst for Lettie— and never a man! Not even a cousin! "I'm so sorry I kept you waiting. I didn't know you were here. Not until this very moment." Then, remembering that she was, after all, Lettie Briggs, she became lofty. "But I don't think we have been introduced."

"My name's Boltwood," said the sandy-haired man. "I'm the detective sent by Mrs. Tisdale to find out what you know about the disappearance of your teacher."

Lettie's jaw dropped. She uttered a bleat of consternation. The guilty recollection that she had broken into Miss Tisdale's study at night flashed through her mind.

"A—a detective!" she blurted. Then, very much frightened, she turned and fled from the room, as terrified as if the innocent Mr. Boltwood had just threatened her with a term in jail.

But in her ears rang a peal of laughter.

Jean, standing outside the library doorway, had overheard the detective's words and had witnessed Lettie's frantic flight. Lettie looked back, her face crimson. She realized that she had been tricked, but just how she did not know. But she did not stop to find out. Jean was still enjoying the joke when Louise came downstairs a moment later.

The girls found Mr. Boltwood looking very much bewildered when they entered the library. The detective was coming to the conclusion that a girls' school was a most extraordinary place indeed. Louise, however, soon put him at his ease, and he sat down to discuss the case in which they were all interested.

Mr. Boltwood had little information to give them. It was his opinion that Miss Tisdale had gone away of her own accord. Jean and Louise told him that they had reason to believe otherwise. To prove their statement, they told him of the existence of Mrs. Brixton, and of the messages she had received from Miss Tisdale. The man was frankly astonished.

"You've made a great deal of progress," he admitted. "Of course, you've had better opportunities of getting information than I. But I think you're treading on very dangerous ground. Don't you think you had better give up the case and leave it to me?"

Louise had decided to say nothing about the contents of the last message received by Mrs.

Brixton, and now she was glad she had with-held this bit of news. It was evident that Mr. Boltwood was eager to solve the mystery him-self and receive all the credit. However, having promised Mrs. Tisdale that they would co-operate with the detective, she did not feel that they were quite justified in holding back all their information.

"It hasn't been very dangerous so far," she said. "We think Miss Tisdale is hidden some place not very far from Hilton, and we all ought to try to find her."

"Not far from Hilton, eh?" mused the de-tective. "Well, you don't solve cases that way. Too much guesswork. What we want is defi-nite information. I'd advise you to leave this strictly to me."

"We're determined to find Miss Tisdale," said Jean, rather annoyed at the man's atti-tude. "Three heads are better than one, don't you think?"

"Sometimes," grunted Mr. Boltwood, and took his departure. "I'm warning you, though, you're treading on thin ice if you get mixed up in this case."

"Perhaps he is right," said Jean, after the detective had gone. "Maybe we should have turned over all our clues to him and let him handle it alone."

Louise shook her head.

"After going this far, we can't give up," she

said. "We didn't tell him about Mr. Tepper and we didn't tell him about the speedboat, but if we don't make any progress, we can still give him that information. Just now, I have an idea. Come up to the study."

When they reached their rooms, Louise spread out the map they had taken from Miss Tisdale's room.

"Here is the river," she said, indicating it on the sheet before them. "And here is the bridge where the road crosses. Now, we went upstream about three miles to the place where we saw the speedboat anchored. Where's the ruler?"

On the map she measured off the space according to scale until she found the approximate place where they had seen the speedboat.

"Why, it isn't far from that side road there leading off the highway!" exclaimed Jean, pointing to a thin black line.

By the chart they could see that the spot indicated on the river was about three miles from Hilton. A side road led off the highway not far from the river in through a farming community. It did not continue to the water but ended at a forest.

"If we go down that road," said Louise, "and then branch off through the woods toward the river we should come out at the place where we saw the boat."

"I'm game to try it. But we'll have a long

walk. We'll have to leave the car at the end of the highway and go the rest of the way on foot. We can't do it today."

Just then Louise happened to glance out of the window. She saw the headmistress, clad in a riding habit, walking toward the stables at the rear of the school.

"The very thing!" she exclaimed, jumping up. "Mrs. Crandall is probably getting a horse. Let's ask her to come with us, and we'll ride through the woods."

They ran downstairs and overtook Mrs. Crandall at the stables, where Zeke Daly was saddling a handsome mare for the principal. Hastily the Dana girls explained that they had discovered a possible clue to Miss Tisdale's whereabouts.

"Will you come with us, Mrs. Crandall?" they begged. "We should be able to reach the place within an hour."

"And if I'm with you I can't very well scold you if we're late for dinner," smiled Mrs. Crandall. "Very well. Run along and change your clothes. I'll wait."

The girls hurried back to change to warm breeches and sweaters, while Zeke saddled their horses. They were elated over their good fortune in obtaining the aid of the head of Starhurst, for they knew they would never have received permission to go scouting alone in the vicinity of the river.

They were soon clattering down the highway. As they rode, Louise explained to Mrs. Crandall that they wished to investigate a mysterious craft they had found anchored in the river. They spoke about Miss Tisdale's code message to her sister, in which she told of being held prisoner in a lonely spot within five miles of Hilton.

"The man in the speedboat must have gone somewhere," said Louise, "and the country back of that side road is about as desolate and lonely as you can imagine."

"I don't see why Mr. Tisdale doesn't call in the police!" declared Mrs. Crandall. "I think his lack of interest in the whole affair is disgraceful."

When they left the highway, they rode out along a rough country lane past a few scattered farmhouses. Mrs. Crandall became dubious when they reached the end of it, on the outskirts of a dark, gloomy forest.

"I'm afraid this is a wild-goose chase," she said. "There can't be any houses farther on."

"I see a trail through the woods," declared Jean. "It probably leads toward the river. Perhaps if we follow it we'll come to the place where we saw the boat."

They went on beneath the creaking branches of the trees, pursuing a path that led them steadily in the direction of the water. The chill November wind swayed the leafless boughs.

The autumn sunlight was too far away to give warmth to the woods.

"Even if we should find the boat," said Mrs. Crandall, "it would be of no advantage to us. I really think we should turn back."

The girls managed to overcome her objections, pointing out that it would be a waste of time to give up the search when they had come so far. A few moments later they were rewarded for their persistence. In the distance, a deep, baying sound broke out on the chill autumn air.

Mrs. Crandall reined in her steed sharply. "What was that?"

"Hounds!" cried Jean excitedly. "They can't be far away, either."

"Where there are hounds," said Louise, "there must be a house. Let's go on."

Their animation was contagious. Even Mrs. Crandall seemed more enthusiastic as they rode on down the rough trail.

The baying of the dogs became louder. Suddenly, as the path wound around a deep clump of trees, they came out on the edge of a clearing. Simultaneously the baying of the animals altered quickly to a series of bloodcurdling howls.

"We've found it!" cried Louise. "There's a house."

The clearing was about three acres in extent. About a hundred yards from the woods was a high wire fence, beyond which stood an old, weather-beaten frame house. In front of the structure were four huge dogs—lean, ferocious brutes, that were creating a terrifying uproar.

"Let's leave our horses here," suggested Jean, dismounting. "I want to get closer to that house. If anyone lives here the dogs will arouse him."

"I don't like the look of those animals!" said Mrs. Crandall, as she climbed reluctantly out of the saddle. "If it wasn't for that fence, I wouldn't set foot on the ground!"

The hounds, howling madly, remained close to the house. Their very presence convinced the Dana girls that the old building sheltered a secret.

Swiftly tethering their horses to the nearby trees, the Dana girls approached the wire fence, followed at a short distance by Mrs. Crandall.

Suddenly, as they came within a few feet of the enclosure, they saw a figure at an open window on the second floor of the house. From where they stood they could recognize the woman who was framed in the opening.

"Miss Tisdale!" gasped Jean.

CHAPTER XIV

A Setback

THEY could scarcely believe their eyes. Yet there was no doubt that the woman who stood in the window of the old house was indeed the missing teacher. It was evident, too, that she recognized them, for she waved and called out to them.

The hounds were setting up such a fearful clamor that Miss Tisdale's words were indistinguishable. She leaned out across the sill, crying to them as loudly as she could, but in the uproar of frenzied howling her voice was lost. To add to the confusion, the animals came racing toward the fence, their fangs bared and their red-rimmed eyes vicious looking. One of the dogs gathered itself for a spring and leaped wildly at the wires. It crashed into the network and fell back, having missed the top by a few inches.

"We'll never be able to reach her as long as those dogs are on guard!" exclaimed Louise.

"They would tear us limb from limb," said Mrs. Crandall nervously. "I think we'd better go back. I really do. I'm afraid one of those brutes will succeed in getting over the fence.''

The animals, goaded to fury, were making frantic efforts to clear the fence. Enraged by repeated failures they created a deafening uproar as they leaped and crashed, howling, against the wires.

Miss Tisdale gestured helplessly and again called out to them, but finally she gave up the attempt, for the clamorous howling of the dogs drowned her words.

''I'll try the sign language!'' cried Jean, holding up her hands and making motions with her fingers such as deaf mutes use.

The teacher shook her head.

''She doesn't understand the signals,'' said Louise, disappointed.

Just then one of the most ferocious of the brutes bounded back into the yard, wheeled, then raced toward the fence at top speed. In mid-flight he sprang. His lean, gray body shot through the air as he leaped toward the top of the wires.

Mrs. Crandall screamed in fear. It seemed that the hound was about to succeed in clearing the fence. The horses, tethered at the edge of the clearing, were snorting and plunging with terror.

The hound's forelegs struck the topmost wire. It clawed desperately for a foothold, then fell back with a snarl of baffled rage.

"We had better go for help," decided Louise. "That brute is coming too close for comfort."

Mrs. Crandall was already untethering her mare, protesting that she did not intend to stay another moment. "We'll be torn to pieces if we remain here!" she declared. "That fence isn't high enough."

They lost no time in mounting their horses. The girls endeavored to signal to Miss Tisdale that they planned to go for help, but whether or not she understood their frantic gestures they could not tell. Soon they were riding wildly back through the woods and out onto the road.

"We certainly have a case for the police!" contended Mrs. Crandall.

"Let's go to Penfield and get help," suggested Jean.

"But at least we've located Miss Tisdale," said Louise, elated. "And she must be there alone, because we saw no one else around the house."

The Dana girls felt a thrill of triumph. They had solved the mystery! Their deductions had been correct and they had found Miss Tisdale's hiding place. They had scarcely expected such a happy conclusion to their afternoon's quest, and were filled with delight when they anticipated the teacher's release as soon as aid could be brought.

They rode hard and fast to Starhurst. When they arrived there, they hastily turned their snorting, perspiring animals over to Zeke Daly and got into the blue coupé. Mrs. Crandall, now as excited as the girls, kept urging them to hurry.

"To the police station!" she ordered. "We can't afford to waste any time."

The sergeant in charge at the Penfield head-quarters was bewildered by the story that a Starhurst teacher was being held prisoner, and needed help immediately. He wanted to delay proceedings by demanding a complete and de-tailed account of all the circumstances, but Louise pleaded for haste.

"We haven't time to explain," she said. "We want action. Please send some patrol-men out to the river with us right away and help us to release Miss Tisdale."

"Tell them to bring whips with them," ad-vised Mrs. Crandall. "There are four of the most bloodthirsty hounds I have ever seen in my life, and they'll have to be beaten off before we can get near the house."

"Hounds!" blurted the astonished officer.

"We'll lead the way in the coupé," Jean an-nounced.

Overridden in his objections, the sergeant detailed half a dozen husky patrolmen to fol-low Mrs. Crandall and the Dana girls in the police car. The officers armed themselves with

heavy whips for the purpose of beating off the
dogs.   None of them had a clear idea of the
purpose of the journey, save that it was to
rescue a teacher who had somehow become im-
prisoned in a house surrounded by dogs.   In a
few minutes, however, the coupé was speeding
out of Penfield, with the uniformed men close
behind.

Louise and Jean were afire with anxiety and
suspense.   They had seen Miss Tisdale, but
she was not yet released from her strange
prison.   Many things could have happened to
her since the trio had ridden away from the
sinister house in the woods, and they could
hardly wait to get back.

It was late in the afternoon, with twilight
closing in, when they reached the end of the
road and struck out through the timberland toward the clearing.   The policemen took the
lead after the Dana girls had shown them the
trail, and plunged ahead at a brisk gait.

"I have a feeling," said Louise presently,
"that something has gone wrong."

"Why do you say that?" asked Mrs. Crandall.

"I think we shan't find Miss Tisdale after
all."   Her lips trembled slightly.

"Nonsense.   There was no one around the
place when we saw her.   As long as the policemen can drive those dogs away——"

"I don't hear the dogs!" exclaimed Jean

Such was the case. On their previous approach they had noticed the deep baying of the hounds while they were still in the woods. Now a heavy silence prevailed, broken only by the snapping and crackling of twigs as the officers plunged through the undergrowth.

"That *is* strange," Mrs. Crandall agreed. "Those dogs should be in a perfect frenzy by now." She was frankly puzzled.

They went on down the trail to the very edge of the clearing, yet there was still no sound of any hounds. Two or three of the patrolmen were already scrambling over the fence.

"Thought you said there were some wild dogs around here, Ma'am," called one of the men in a brusque voice.

"There were!" insisted Mrs. Crandall. "They tried to jump over the fence to get at us."

Louise and Jean anxiously eyed the old house. There was not a sign of life. They sought the window at which they had seen Miss Tisdale—it was closed. The spot looked as if it had been deserted for years.

"Are you sure this is the right place?" asked another patrolman. "There doesn't seem to be anyone around."

"There *must* be!" exclaimed Jean desperately. "Why, it isn't an hour since we were here. We saw Miss Tisdale at the window. She tried to shout to us.

The officers shrugged their shoulders. It was plain that they were beginning to doubt the whole story.

"We'll take a look around," said their leader. "But I think you must have dreamed about those dogs."

The policemen crossed the lawn and went directly up to the house. The hounds did not appear. Two of the men tried the door of the building and stepped inside.

CHAPTER XV

ANOTHER MESSAGE

AFTER a short while the two policemen emerged.

"Why, the place is empty," one of them said. "There isn't a sign of anyone here."

The Dana girls were crestfallen, for this was a crushing disappointment to them. It was plain now that the teacher's captors must have been somewhere near the house on the previous occasion, and that they had lost no time in moving their prisoner to another place of concealment.

"That's a fine trip to take for nothing," growled one of the patrolmen in disgust. "What was the idea? A practical joke?"

"Practical joke!" exclaimed Mrs. Crandall, who was just as bewildered and disappointed as the Dana girls. "No indeed. We *saw* her, and we saw the dogs, too. They even tried to bite us. If you men will get busy and look around, you may find her yet."

The patrolmen dispersed, but Louise could hear them muttering something about "excitable females," and exchanging remarks to the effect that the whole affair was a "pipe dream." She could hardly blame them for being skeptical, for the place looked as if it had been deserted for months. The policemen searched the grounds in the rear of the deserted house, even exploring the brush around the clearing, but without success. Finally, in the gathering gloom, they announced they could do no more.

"I don't know what it's all about," said the leader of the men, "but if somebody was held in that building, she's been taken away. You were probably seen when you came up to the fence the first time. Maybe if you'll give us a little more information——"

Louise and Jean decided, however, to keep further details to themselves. They knew they were undertaking a heavy responsibility, but they were prepared to do that for the sake of the Tisdales. This search, they realized, was not without peril. What unseen eyes had been watching them while they were trying to communicate with Miss Tisdale on their first visit to the clearing? Had they been observed? Had they been identified? And if they had been recognized, would the teacher's captors seek revenge for the enforced flight from the old house?

The girls were worried, for they felt that now they were certainly in danger. However, they said nothing about it to the officers, who were making no secret of their resentment at the outcome of the journey. Mrs. Crandall was nonplussed.

"They spirited her away. No doubt of that," she said. "But what did they do with the dogs? I can't understand it. And where did they go?"

"I think they escaped by boat," ventured Jean, her eyes flashing with excitement. "This place isn't very far from the river. If they had gone through the woods, the policemen would have picked up their trail."

The afternoon had ended ingloriously. It had grown dark and dreary, casting a shadow of gloom into the girls' spirits. They returned to the school, silent and crestfallen. The setback discouraged them for only a while, however, for Jean optimistically pointed out that they had made some progress at least.

"If we could find Miss Tisdale once, we can find her again," she said in a determined voice. "We made a mistake in leaving the place. One of us should have stayed on guard while the others went for help."

"Don't forget the dogs," Louise reminded her sister. "By the way, I think we had better tell Mrs. Tisdale about it. Perhaps we made a mistake in holding some of the facts back from Mr. Boltwood. He might have had better luck if we had told him everything."

That evening they reached the teacher's

mother by phone and told her their story. She was greatly distressed when she learned that her daughter's captors had slipped through the hands of the police, but she praised highly the Dana girls for their work. She promised to tell the detective the whole story, in the hope that he might be able to pick up the trail.

"Something will have to be done soon," Mrs. Tisdale added. "My husband is becoming suspicious. He is wondering why Amy hasn't been out to see us and why we haven't heard from her. Tonight he was speaking of going to Starhurst himself, but I'm doing all I can to delay him."

"If he were to go, there's no telling what might happen," mused Louise as she turned away from the telephone. "If he should come to Starhurst, he'd learn everything and would want to know why he hadn't been told."

Mrs. Tisdale was evidently successful in her efforts to keep her husband away from Starhurst, for he did not put in an appearance at the school the next day. When the afternoon classes were over, the Dana girls lost no time in taking the blue coupé out of the garage and driving toward Hilton, where it was their intention to call on Mrs. Brixton and tell her what had happened.

"Besides," said Louise, "she may have received another letter."

"It's strange that the messages have indicated that five thousand dollars must be paid, and yet have given no instructions telling how the money should be turned over."

"That's why I think there will be another note."

Louise was correct in her surmise, for when they arrived at Lone Tree Cottage they found Mrs. Brixton in a highly excited state over a letter that had arrived in the afternoon mail.

"It came just a half hour ago!" she exclaimed breathlessly, the paper fluttering in her hand. "It's from Amy. She has been moved."

"We know that," said Jean.

Quickly she explained how they had found the house in the clearing and had seen Miss Tisdale, whereupon they had gone back to Penfield for help, only to find the house deserted upon their return.

"What is in the letter?" asked Louise, who was now being hugged violently by Baby Faith. "Does she state where she is now?"

Mrs. Brixton showed them the message. It was quite lengthy and, in substance, instructed Mrs. Brixton to go to her father and demand five thousand dollars in cash, which was to be paid over for the safe return of Miss Tisdale. The instructions were to the effect that the money should be mailed to one "Jacob Jacobs, c/o General Delivery, Oak Falls," or harm would come to the missing teacher.

"Oak Falls!" exclaimed the Danas in amazement. "Why, that's the town where we live!"

"Do you come from Oak Falls?" queried Mrs. Brixton.

"Yes. They must have taken Miss Tisdale there."

"Her code message says she has been moved."

By reading every fourth word of the note the girls divined Miss Tisdale's secret instructions.

These words, when separated from the original letter, ran as follows:

". . . have . . . been . . . moved . . . do . . . not . . . ask . . . father . . . for . . . money . . . will . . . still . . . try . . . to . . . escape . . . my . . . captor . . . is . . . a . . . coward . . . will . . . not . . . harm . . . me . . ."

"She still insists that the ransom isn't to be paid!" said Jean.

"Just the same," declared Louise, "we should send a letter to Oak Falls—a dummy letter. We can have the post office watched, and when this man who calls himself 'Jacob Jacobs' comes there, he'll be caught."

"We'll tell Uncle Ned!" cried Jean.

"He'll be able to help us. We'll get in touch with him at once."

CHAPTER XVI

UNCLE NED ON GUARD

ALTHOUGH the girls had been disappointed the night before, they were now radiantly jubilant. By frightening Miss Tisdale's captor from his hiding place in the abandoned house, they had forced him to take some definite action toward collecting the ransom money. It would be a simple matter, they felt, for Uncle Ned to have the Oak Falls post office watched. When "Jacob Jacobs" should appear to collect his letter, he could be seized instantly and compelled to divulge the present whereabouts of the missing teacher.

They telephoned their guardian as soon as they returned to Starhurst, for they had a great deal to tell him about their adventures of the previous evening. They learned in turn that Uncle Ned had not been idle in regard to the mystery.

"I checked up on the firm of Brixton and Tepper," he said, "and got some information from a marine agency I know. They tell me there is no truth whatsoever in Tepper's story and that the affairs of the company were in

142

good shape. Brixton's reputation was first rate, but Tepper is known to have been mixed up in a number of shady deals outside of the life preserver business, and since Brixton's death has gone bankrupt.''

When the girls told him about the ransom letter, Uncle Ned was surprised that the trail had led to Oak Falls, and appeared more eager than ever to get to the bottom of the investigation.

"Why should they ask that the money be sent here?" he demanded. "Of course, Tepper may have come to Oak Falls. I imagine he will turn out to be 'Jacob Jacobs'—when we catch him."

"Will you see that the post office is watched?" asked Louise.

"Indeed I will," promised Uncle Ned. "I'll have the clerks keep an eye open for that dummy letter when it arrives. You had better write it out tonight and mail it. Then I'll watch the general delivery window myself. If this 'Jacob Jacobs' shows up, I'll collar him. Just a minute. Your aunt wants to speak to you." He held out the receiver to her.

Aunt Harriet, sister of Uncle Ned, acted as housekeeper of his home on the outskirts of Oak Falls. She was a second mother to the Dana girls, always kind and thoughtful of their needs. In a moment Louise heard her pleasant voice on the wire.

"Hello, dear," said her relative. "Do you realize that Thanksgiving will be along in a few days?"

"To tell you the truth," laughed Louise, "we have been so busy we have not realized Thanksgiving will be here soon."

"You must have a lot on your minds to forget about a vacation. Now, I want you girls to forsake this mystery of yours for a few days and come home for Thanksgiving. I've been counting on it."

Louise hesitated. "She wants us home for Thanksgiving," she whispered to Jean.

"How about Miss Tisdale?"

Aunt Harriet must have guessed the object of the conference, for she said:

"Now, stop worrying about that secret you're trying to clear up. Your uncle has been telling me about it, but just the same I don't think you should stay at Starhurst during your vacation."

"Why, of course we'll come," agreed Louise. "We wouldn't miss Thanksgiving with you for anything. Perhaps the mystery will be cleared up by that time, anyway."

"Let's hope so. I never saw such girls for getting mixed up in affairs that have nothing to do with school work."

"It makes school work all the more exciting," laughed Jean into the telephone.

"No doubt." returned their aunt drily. "But

I haven't seen you since the summer holidays.
I'll ask your uncle to drive up to Starhurst
for you and bring you back.''

''When will he come?''

There was a brief colloquy between Aunt
Harriet and Uncle Ned.

''He says he'll try to drive up tomorrow
evening. I really think he is just as excited
about this trouble as you are, and he'll help
you with the case until vacation begins.''

''Oh, that will be great!'' said Louise. ''We
couldn't ask for anything better than that.''

''Maybe I'll bring this fellow 'Jacob Jacobs'
along with me,'' broke in the deep voice of
Uncle Ned, a hint of assurance in his tones.

When the girls went to bed that night they
were so excited they could hardly fall asleep.
They had addressed a large envelope to ''Jacob
Jacobs, c/o General Delivery, Oak Falls,'' according to the instructions in the letter, and
had mailed it in time to catch the night mail
train to their home town. The envelope contained nothing except a few blank sheets of
paper, but they felt that this trap would be
sufficient to bring ''Jacob Jacobs'' to grief.

''He'll think it contains five one-thousand
dollar bills,'' said Jean, a look of anticipation
in her blue eyes.

But Louise was not so confident.

''He may be more clever than we imagine,
and suspect that the general delivery window

will be watched,'' and her face looked a trifle
worried at the thought.

''But the message said Miss Tisdale would
be harmed if the money wasn't sent. Perhaps
he thinks that will save him.''

''Well, it's up to Uncle Ned now,'' replied
Louise. So the girls decided to leave the matter in his hands for the time being.

They heard nothing from their uncle next
morning, and during classes all that day were
in a state of suspense, wondering if ''Jacob
Jacobs'' had fallen into the trap. No message
had been received yet when the last period was
over for the afternoon.

''We'll have to wait until Uncle Ned arrives,'' sighed Louise. ''Maybe he'll bring
'Jacob Jacobs' with him, as he said he would!''

''All nailed up in a crate like a chicken, in
the back of the car,'' laughed Jean.

''Speaking of chicken—I'm afraid poor Mrs.
Brixton and Baby Faith won't have a very
luxurious Thanksgiving dinner. She told me
yesterday that most of the money Mrs. Tisdale
sent her had to go toward the rent.''

''No Thanksgiving dinner! Oh, we can't let
that happen! She is sorrowful enough.''

''I suppose she isn't feeling very thankful
just now, either,'' said Louise. ''Nevertheless,
we might present her with a chicken.''

''Why stop at chicken? Turkey! We'll buy
her a turkey——''

"And all the trimmings. Let's go right away and make up a big basket. One of the stores downtown has the most luscious looking ones I've ever seen," said Jean triumphantly.

In a food shop some little distance from the school the Dana girls inspected a tempting array of baskets of all sizes, listed at various prices. They finally selected one containing a big, fat turkey, a generous supply of groceries, and an array of fruits and delicacies that made their mouths water. The purchase took most of their pocket money, but they did not mind that. The thought of Mrs. Brixton's delight was sufficient compensation, and they proudly carried the huge gift back to the school, placing it in their study.

"Won't she be glad!" said Jean. "Thanksgiving just doesn't seem like Thanksgiving without a turkey."

"I shouldn't be able to eat a bite of my Thanksgiving dinner at Uncle Ned's if I thought Mrs. Brixton didn't have enough food in her house."

As the evening meal would not be served for some time, the girls decided to drive out to call on Mrs. Tisdale in the hope that she might have received some further word from her detective. They appreciated her burden of anxiety, and hoped, too, that they might relieve her worries somewhat by telling her of the trap they had set for "Jacob Jacobs."

"It will be a sad Thanksgiving for her if Miss Tisdale isn't soon found," said Louise, as they drove through Penfield.

"And what a glorious day if we do locate her!" declared Jean, who insisted upon looking on the bright side of everything. "I only hope Uncle Ned has good news for us when he comes."

When they arrived at the Tisdale home, they realized immediately that unless they succeeded in clearing up the mystery very soon there would be two invalids at the place instead of one. Mrs. Tisdale looked even more careworn and worried than she had on their previous visit. Her face was haggard and pale, and her voice trembled when she spoke. She confessed that she had been unable to eat or sleep to amount to anything since she had first learned of her daughter's disappearance.

"I can't keep the secret much longer," she finally told the girls brokenly, tears welling up in her eyes. "I'll have to tell Mr. Tisdale, no matter what the consequences may be. I want to see Alice and the baby—and I want Amy."

"Will you come with us to Hilton tomorrow?" said Jean quickly, endeavoring to keep the distracted mother from breaking down.

"Oh, I should love to," said the harassed woman. "And yet—I can't bear to deceive Mr. Tisdale—but I don't dare tell him——"

"Where is he now?" asked Louise.

"He's in the sun porch, reading. But surely you're not going to tell him?" asked Mrs. Tisdale, frightened. "You mustn't. The shock might be too great for him."

"I shan't tell him," promised Louise. "But I want to talk to him. I'm going to put another idea or two into his mind, so it will make things easier when his forgiveness is asked. I begin to think he is not as set in his ideas as he pretends to be."

CHAPTER XVII

Two Plans That Failed

Louise's conversation with old Mr. Tisdale was brief, because the Danas were eager to return to Starhurst and meet Uncle Ned. When she began her drive back to the school, she was in decidedly high spirits.

"What did he say?" asked Jean curiously.

"I didn't tell him anything, of course," replied Louise. "I just sounded him out on the general idea of forgiveness. He's a gruff old gentleman, but I think he is not nearly as cantankerous as he pretends to be. He even admitted that a man of his age should be on good terms with the whole world because he might have to leave it soon. Then I asked him if he were on good terms with everybody, but he wouldn't answer me."

"That will give him something to ponder over," observed Jean thoughtfully. "I believe we'll soon be able to tell him about Mrs. Brixton. At that, I doubt if it would hurt him if we were to do it now. It's pretty hard to carry a grudge that long."

"If it wasn't for Mrs. Tisdale, I would tell

150

him. But he has complained about his health for so long that she is quite convinced any sort of shock would kill him. By the way, is Mrs. Tisdale coming with us to see Mrs. Brixton tomorrow?"

"I had to argue with her to convince her it would be all right. She's afraid to leave Mr. Tisdale alone, but I told her that Uncle Ned would stay with him," said Jean.

"Good idea! Speaking of Uncle Ned, I wonder if he has reached Starhurst yet? I'm going to step on the gas," and soon the girls were racing down the road toward the school.

When they entered the building, they found that Uncle Ned had not yet put in an appearance, and had not telephoned. Another kind of surprise awaited them, however, as they reached their study. The precious Thanksgiving basket which they had bought for Mrs. Brixton was standing in the middle of the table. Upon removing the cover to inspect the good things they had provided for the feast for the young widow and her little girl, they had a disagreeable shock.

The turkey was gone! The groceries were gone! The oranges and apples were gone! The basket instead was filled with rocks and old newspapers.

The girls gazed at the receptacle in outright dismay.

"What a low, mean trick!" exclaimed Louise

at last, her face betraying her anger. "Someone has stolen every bit of that lovely Thanksgiving dinner!"

"It's our own fault," declared Jean remorsefully. "We should have locked our study door."

"I suppose this is one of Lettie Briggs's so-called jokes."

Jean began to regret that she had tricked Lettie into meeting the detective in the library. Although they had no proof that she was responsible for the disappearance of the food, they had a strong conviction that no other girl in the school would play such a trick on them.

"She did it to pay us back for the scare she got when she met Mr. Boltwood. I suppose we *are* one ahead of Lettie in the matter of jokes——"

"As long as she doesn't waste the food, I don't mind," said Louise philosophically. "Perhaps she'll give it to some poor family."

"Not Lettie."

Evelyn Starr happened to enter the study just then, looking very girlish in a blue sport dress, a band of ribbon about her bobbed hair.

"Why the rock samples?" she asked, noticing the basket. "Are you taking a course in geology?"

"We bought a Thanksgiving dinner for a widow——" began Louise.

"Thanksgiving dinner for a widow! You

must be out of your minds. Rocks—newspapers——"

"There *was* a turkey," said Jean ruefully.

Evelyn nodded understandingly, as the truth
dawned upon her.

"So! Well, such things will happen." She
moved toward the door, then glanced back. "I
think I'll drop in and see Lettie and Ina for a
while. Maybe I'll get some information," and
she nodded her head as if she had found the
guilty parties.

"Whenever a particularly mean trick is
played in Starhurst," said Louise, as Evelyn
disappeared, "everyone immediately thinks of
Lettie Briggs."

"And the guess is usually right," added
Jean. "I hope Evelyn catches her eating the
apples."

Presently the dinner gong sounded, so the
girls went down to the dining hall a trifle disappointed. Lettie Briggs and Ina Mason were
giggling and whispering together, and seemed
to have a very amusing secret between them.
As the Dana girls had no proof of their guilt,
they could say nothing. Louise, however, told
the girls at the table about the missing Thanksgiving dinner.

"It's really too bad," she said, "because the
food was for a poor widow and her little girl,
and now we haven't enough money to buy another basket."

From all around the table came expressions of deep feeling and sympathy for the poor woman and child, and censure for the guilty ones. "What a shame!" . . . "It should be reported to Mrs. Crandall." . . . "A person who would play a trick like that ought to be put on bread and water for a week!"

So unanimous were the other girls in their condemnation of those implicated that Lettie and Ina were rather conspicuous because of their silence. Somewhat belatedly Lettie said: "I think it's a dreadfully mean trick," while Ina added hastily:

"Yes, I think so too."

"You would!" remarked Jean tartly. "But you're a bit late with your sympathy."

Lettie flushed. Ina glared. None of the others at the table had the slightest doubt as to the identity of the culprits.

The mystery of the vanished dinner was forgotten when the girls left the dining room and went back upstairs. Waiting for them in their study they found Captain Ned Dana, reading a newspaper by the light of the study lamp and looking as if he had been comfortably ensconced there for hours.

The girls flung themselves upon him in delight, and hugged him until he begged to be set free. Finally he sat up, smoothing his rumpled hair.

"Well, I suppose you want to know all about

'Jacob Jacobs' and whether I brought him along with me.''

"Did you?" cried Jean. "Did he call for the letter, Uncle Ned?"

Captain Dana made a rueful face, showing that his news was disappointing.

"He was too smart for that. He got the letter all right, but he didn't call for it. No, I didn't lay my hands on Mr. Jacob Jacobs."

"But how did he get the letter?" they asked him in one breath, anxiety and wonder in their voices.

"Well," said Uncle Ned, "I told the people at the post office to be on the lookout for a letter addressed to 'Jacob Jacobs,' and the man at the general delivery window said he would put it aside and give me some sort of a signal whenever anyone asked for it. So I stood over by the door and watched everybody who called there for mail.

"Finally, at about half-past ten, along came a ragged little boy. He walked up to the window and I didn't pay any particular attention to him. I was waiting for a *man*, of course, and I happened to be looking out into the street at the time. When I turned around, the little fellow was just going out the door, and the clerk was waving to me. 'That's the one!' he was saying. 'He got the letter.'

"Well, you can imagine how surprised I was. 'What?' I said. 'Is that Jacob Jacobs?' 'He said he was sent to get any mail for Jacob Jacobs,' the man at the window said. So I ran out of the post office as fast as I could, and was just in time to see the boy scuttling around the corner. I went after him but he cut across the street and got lost in the crowd, and there I stood feeling like an old bungler.''

Captain Dana looked so crestfallen when he explained how he had been outwitted by Jacob Jacobs and the youngster, that the girls hastened to sympathize with him. Nevertheless, they were deeply disappointed, for they had hoped that the bogus letter would surely bring about a capture.

''So now,'' said Uncle Ned heavily, ''it looks as if we'll have to start all over again. When Jacob Jacobs finds that there isn't any money in the envelope, he won't try that method again.''

''It's too bad,'' said Louise. ''However, it can't be helped.''

''What's the plan for tomorrow?'' asked Uncle Ned. ''I'm getting interested in this affair. You'll have your classes, of course, but what's the program when school is out?''

''We want to drive Mrs. Tisdale out to Hilton. She is very eager to meet her daughter and the baby. But in the meantime,'' explained Jean, ''someone will have to stay with Mr. Tisdale——''

''And I'm the man for the job,'' declared

Uncle Ned. "I'll read up on a couple of patent medicine almanacs tomorrow and by the time I'm through with him, he'll have learned all about a dozen new diseases and ailments that he never knew existed."

Later, as the girls were preparing for bed, Louise ventured to express her anxiety about their scheme for the following day.

"There's no telling what will happen when poor Alice Brixton and her mother meet," she said.

CHAPTER XVIII

The Missing Child

Uncle Ned was as good as his word. When he and the girls drove out to the home of their teacher the following afternoon, the worthy skipper received a warm greeting and breath-taking handclasp from Mr. Tisdale. Within ten minutes time the pair were seated on the sun perch, deep in an earnest and animated discussion on some apparently important topic. When Mrs. Tisdale intruded for a moment to explain to her husband that she was going for "a little drive" with the Dana girls, her husband waved her aside impatiently with his hand.

"Go ahead!" he cried. "Go ahead! Captain Dana and I are very busy. Now, Captain, there is a very peculiar thing about this trouble of mine. Most victims complain of spots before the eyes——"

Mrs. Tisdale withdrew, and left him with his pet subject. The girls were delighted that she had managed to break away so easily. "I don't know what we should have done without Uncle Ned," said Louise, as they drove away.

158

In her happiness and relief at the prospect of at last meeting her long-lost daughter and the grandchild she had never seen, Mrs. Tisdale seemed less worried and careworn, despite the fact that the mystery of the teacher's disappearance was as far from being solved as ever. "I owe so much to you girls," she told them gratefully. "If it hadn't been for you, I should never have learned about Alice and Baby Faith——"

They drove through Penfield, out past Starhurst, and then onto the main highway. The city had been left behind, and Louise was racing along at a lively speed when suddenly she heard a cry from Jean as a car passed them on the road.

"Louise! Quick! Do you recognize that car we just saw?"

The elder Dana girl had paid scant attention to the machine as it had gone by, but now she studied it closely as it sped on ahead of them. The auto seemed somehow familiar. Then she remembered. The scene at the barricade on the Hilton road during their vain pursuit of Mr. Tepper flashed through her mind.

"Tepper's car!" she cried.

Louise pressed down on the accelerator and the coupé leaped ahead. Mrs. Tisdale, somewhat alarmed by their sudden excitement and by the unusual burst of speed, held onto the edge of her seat to keep her balance.

"Don't worry," Jean assured her. "If that's Mr. Tepper and if we can catch him, it may mean the end of the mystery."

The chase, however, did not last long. The car ahead slowed down and pulled over in front of the next gasoline station. A woman stepped out and spoke to the attendant. As the girls drove slowly past, they saw that the vehicle had no other occupant.

"We're wrong," shrugged Louise. "But it certainly does look like the car we followed that afternoon."

They soon forgot the incident, and in due course of time arrived at Hilton and drove up in front of Lone Tree Cottage. Mrs. Tisdale was very excited, clasping and unclasping her hands constantly.

"Is—is this the place where—where my Alice lives?" she asked with a tremor in her voice. "It's such a—a lonesome place."

The girls gently assisted the quivering woman from the coupé, and just as her feet touched the ground the door of the little house was flung open and Mrs. Brixton rushed down the path.

"Mother!" she cried.

"Alice! My own Alice!"

Mother and daughter were clasped in each other's arms, weeping tears of joy. It was a touching and affectionate meeting, this reunion of these two who had not seen each other for years, and the Dana girls tactfully decided to leave them to themselves for the time being.

"You'll have a great deal to say to each other," said Louise to Alice Brixton. "Where is Baby Faith? Your mother will be overjoyed to see her. We'll find her."

"She went up to the store a little while ago with the woman who lives across the street."

"We'll go and look for her," offered Jean.

There was very little to explore. The village was small, and around the bend in the road they discovered a general store which apparently supplied its inhabitants with most of the necessities of life. Baby Faith and the neighbor woman were not in the shop, so the girls were obliged to wait for about ten minutes. The solitary clerk was showing numerous spades and shovels to a grouchy old gentleman who finally went away without buying anything.

"Baby Faith Brixton?" asked the clerk, when he was finally able to give them his attention. "Oh, she was in here quite a while ago. Half an hour, I'd say. They went back down the road."

"She has probably been in the neighbor's house all this time," laughed Jean, as they left the store. However, when they called at the dwelling across the road from Lone Tree Cottage and informed the neighbor that they were looking for Baby Faith, the girls learned that the child had not been there. The talkative woman was instantly concerned.

"I've been baking ever since we returned from the store," she said. "Faith came home with me, but not into the house. She was playing around in the back yard."

But the back yard was deserted.

"Well, that's strange!" declared the woman, greatly flustered. "She was there not ten minutes ago, for I looked out the kitchen window and saw her. Do you suppose she could have gone up into the woods—where she went the day she was lost?"

Afraid that Baby Faith might have wandered away again, the Dana girls hastened up the path into the woods. Although they called the child's name time and again they heard no answering cry. The neighbor, in the meantime, was exploring the village street. By the time the girls returned to her house no trace of the child had been found by any of them.

"I can't understand it!" declared the woman, wringing her hands, and apparently all unstrung. "I feel responsible, in a way, but when I saw her playing out in the yard—and Hilton is such a small place, after all—oh, dear, how can I face the child's mother? She'll be simply frantic if anything has happened——"

"She may have gone into some other house," Louise suggested sensibly. "There is no cause for being so upset. She'll turn up all right. We'll make inquiries.''

The woman went with them as they called at some of the other places on the street. But their search was fruitless. No one, apparently, had seen Baby Faith within the past quarter of an hour, leaving the trio in a decided quandary.

At length, however, a tousle-headed little boy ran up to them.

''Are you looking for Baby Faith?'' he asked, licking industriously on a big stick of candy. ''She went away.''

''Went away?'' said Louise quickly. ''Where? Into the woods?''

''No. She rode off in a car. I saw her,'' he affirmed, looking very proud at being able to give them this information.

The girls were overcome by a dreadful conviction.

''A big car?'' demanded Jean. ''A closed car?''

The boy nodded, his eyes large as saucers.

''Yes,'' he said. ''A woman was driving it. She asked Baby Faith if she'd like to come for a ride. And they drove away.''

''It was the woman we followed!'' gasped Louise. ''I'm sure of it. And it was Tepper's car after all!''

CHAPTER XIX

MR. TISDALE LEARNS THE TRUTH

THE Dana girls were stunned by this disastrous development. Tepper had struck again—and this time at a defenseless child. Having failed in his efforts to secure payment of the money by keeping Miss Tisdale prisoner, he had determined to bring matters to a head by holding Baby Faith as well. The girls did not doubt but that the woman in the car was an accomplice of the sailor—perhaps his wife —and that she had come to Hilton deliberately with the purpose of taking the child away with her.

"Can't we follow her?" cried Jean desperately.

"We should only waste our time," said Louise. "She has had a good start. We could never pick up the trail of the car now. No, we must tell Mrs. Brixton——"

"I haven't the heart to do it. She will be overcome with grief."

"But she *must* be told. And then, secret or no secret, we must go back and get Mr. Tisdale and Uncle Ned to help us."

The neighbor, conscience-stricken because she had let Baby Faith out of her sight, was badly frightened.

"It's all my fault," she wailed. "It's all my fault. I promised Mrs. Brixton I'd look after the child—and now she's gone. But who would have thought anything like that would happen?"

"It can't be helped now," said Louise, consoling her. "These people were bent on getting possession of Baby Faith, and they would have made some other plan if the woman had failed this time."

Reluctantly they went into Lone Tree Cottage to break the sad news. The task was even more difficult because Mrs. Brixton and her mother were unutterably happy in being reunited after all the long years of separation. As gently as possible, the Dana girls told them their story.

At first Mrs. Brixton seemed stunned, unable to comprehend their meaning. Then, the tragedy of the situation dawning upon her, she sprang to her feet.

"My baby!" she cried. "My baby! They have stolen her! Where is she? Where did they go with her?"

She ran toward the door but the girls restrained her.

"You must be brave," said Louise, placing her hand on the distraught woman. "We'll find her again, never fear. Perhaps they'll think better of it and send her back——"

The young widow struggled wildly, trying to break away from them and rush in mad pursuit of her child. She was like a woman possessed.

"I must find my baby! She's all I have in the world——"

Then the color drained suddenly from her wan cheeks, her body sagged, one hand clutched her throat, and she collapsed in a dead faint Mrs. Tisdale herself was nearly prostrated by the shock. Coming so close upon the joyful reunion with her daughter, the blow was doubly severe. With one stark stroke it had dashed away their happiness.

"You must tell my husband," she said brokenly. "He must help. I know he will help. Whatever these people want—money—anything—we must do what they ask. Anything in the world to have my daughter Amy and my grandchild safely back again!"

The girls were busy attending to Mrs. Brixton, placing her on a couch, chafing her hands, and applying cold water to her face. The neighbor ran to the kitchen for some stimulant. When she returned, she said to the girls:

"I'll stay here and look after the two of them. Don't worry. They'll be all right. You go and get help so you can find Baby Faith for these people."

"The police!" suggested Mrs. Tisdale, who had suddenly sat down in a chair and seemed unable to rise. "Tell the police!"

Louise shook her head.

"That's just what we mustn't do yet. They're holding Faith as a hostage until the money is paid over. We can't take any risks."

"You're quite right," agreed the distracted grandmother. "No harm must come to the child. If they demand money, it must and will be paid."

Leaving the neighbor, anxious to make amends for her neglect, in charge of the house, the Dana girls hurried out to the car.

Up to this time they had obeyed Miss Tisdale's instructions to ignore the demands for ransom. With Baby Faith's disappearance, however, the situation was altered. The teacher had been confident that she would come to no harm, but they could afford to take no such risks where the child was concerned.

"And Tepper knows it!" said Louise bitterly, as they drove back toward Penfield. "Miss Tisdale was right when she said he was a coward."

"If we had only followed that car when we were so sure that it was Tepper's!"

"If we had at least taken the license number——"

"I did," announced Jean calmly.

"You took the number? Oh, good!" exclaimed Louise. "Now we'll have something to work on."

"I didn't jot it down but I remembered it. The car was driving ahead of us for some time, you recall. The number was K-74917. I'll write it down now in case I should forget it."

Louise was cheered by the knowledge that the number of the car, at least, was in their possession. It might be possible to trace its ownership and thereby locate Tepper's present hiding place.

"We can ask the police to look for that machine without telling them why," she said. "Perhaps we ought to stop off at the Penfield headquarters now."

"I think we had better leave that to Uncle Ned," advised Jean.

"And to think we were trying to save Mr. Tisdale from a shock! It'll be a double blow to him now."

When they reached the home of their teacher, however, they found that any blow which their bad news might cause the old gentleman had been greatly lessened by the occurrences of the afternoon visit. Uncle Ned had not been idle. When Mr. Tisdale came down the steps to meet them, his hand on Captain Dana's shoulder, his first words were:

"Young ladies, I believe I owe you an apology. I have let you think that I am a hard-hearted, crusty old man, as vindictive as—as an elephant. Well, I'm not. And I want to thank you for trying to save me from trouble and worry—but I wish you had explained things to me."

"Uncle Ned has told you the secret!" gasped the girls.

Mr. Tisdale nodded.

"He has given me the whole story." Turning to Louise, he said, "You made it easy for him, talking to me as you did. I think you are a very remarkable girl—and your sister, too. And I am ashamed of myself," went on Mr. Tisdale hurriedly, "to think that my two daughters were in terrible trouble, and I was sitting here at home complaining about my health! I've been a proud old idiot, as stubborn as a mule, but I wish to make up for it. For a long time I have wanted to make amends for the wrong I have done, but my obstinacy held me back."

The Danas, utterly surprised, blushed at the compliment.

"You can make amends now," said Louise.

"Your daughter needs you more now than she has ever needed you before," added Jean.

"Why, what's the matter?" demanded Mr. Tisdale. "Is she ill? Has anything happened to the baby?"

"Baby Faith has been stolen!"

Mr. Tisdale's face went white. For a moment the girls were afraid that the shock. they

dreaded and feared had proved to be too great
for him to withstand. He gripped Captain
Dana's arm to steady himself, one hand cov-
ering his eyes as if to blot out some horrible
vision.

"Come!" he said hoarsely. "It may not be
too late. The baby! The baby I have never
seen. The baby I have never even known
about. Stolen, you say? How? By whom?"

"By the same people who spirited Miss Tisdale away."

"We'll run them to earth!" declared the old
man grimly, clenching his fists with a realization of the tragedy confronting his own flesh
and blood. "I'll get my daughter and my
grandchild back if I have to spend the rest of
my life searching for them, and if it takes
every cent I have in the world. Captain Dana,
my car is in the garage. Can you drive?"

"I can," replied Uncle Ned with determination. "And I can drive fast."

"Then let's waste no more time. I have
frittered away too many minutes already.
How did it happen? How was the child
stolen?"

The girls quickly explained the circumstances
of Baby Faith's disappearance. They were
surprised at the sudden change in Mr. Tisdale.
From a querulous, cantankerous old man, concerned only with himself, he had become
repentant and eager to redeem the wrong he

had done. They knew that he would now spare
no resource, even if it meant yielding to the
demands of Sailor Tepper, to restore his daughter and grandchild to him.

Before the day was over, the father, whose
obstinacy had caused so much trouble to himself and to his loved ones, had sought and
received forgiveness in Lone Tree Cottage
from the heartbroken daughter whom he had
once upon a time disowned.

But the family was not as yet complete. Two
other members were needed to fill their cup of
happiness to the brim. Baby Faith and Amy
Tisdale were still missing!

Knowing this, the Dana girls determined to
bend every effort to solve the mystery quickly.
They asked the police to trace car K-74917.
They got in touch with Detective Boltwood,
giving him the news of the latest disappearance. Then they held a council of war.

"I think our next move," suggested Louise,
"should be on the river. I have some ideas
about Tepper and his speedboat."

And so it was decided.

CHAPTER XX

The Speedboat

IT must be confessed that the Dana girls did not shine scholastically the next day. It seemed an eternity until the bell rang for dismissal of classes that afternoon. Throughout the entire session they had been in a near frenzy of impatience and suspense, hoping against hope that Mr. Tisdale, Uncle Ned, and Boltwood, the detective, had somehow succeeded in running the villainous Tepper to earth.

Uncle Ned, who had accepted an invitation to stay at the Tisdale home, had promised to call for his nieces at Starhurst that afternoon. They found him waiting for them at the wheel of the Tisdale family car.

"No luck yet," he said briefly, answering their unspoken inquiry when they came running out to him. "We've obtained a little information but it isn't much. I was half tempted to go out on the river myself to look for that speedboat, but I thought you'd be disappointed if I went without you. So that's where we're heading for now."

"What do you mean, Uncle Ned, when you say you've had some information?" asked Jean, as the girls settled themselves in the roomy front seat beside their uncle.

"Well, I've had a report from a detective I hired in Oak Falls," said Captain Dana, as he backed the big car out of the driveway. "I asked him to hunt around for the boy who got that letter addressed to Jacob Jacobs. And he found him."

"Jacob Jacobs?"

"No. He found the boy. And he made the youngster tell him about the letter. It seems the lad was hired by a man to go to the general delivery window and ask for mail addressed to Jacob Jacobs. And that man," concluded Uncle Ned, "answered the description of Sailor Tepper!"

"I knew it," declared Louise emphatically.

"The boy didn't have much to tell. He said the man was waiting for him on a side street. Jacobs—or Tepper, rather—grabbed the letter, gave the lad a dollar and drove away in a car. The boy remembered the car's number, but we haven't been able to find a trace of it yet."

"What was the number?"

With one hand on the wheel, Uncle Ned rummaged in his pocket for the detective's report. When he found it, he read aloud the number.

"K-74917."

"Why, that's the number of the machine the woman was driving!" cried Jean in excitement. "The one we asked the police to locate."

"The woman who took Baby Faith away," added Louise.

"Well, that proves that Tepper and this woman are in league with each other," said Uncle Ned. "But we practically guessed that, anyway. The thing now is to find out where Tepper is hiding, and where Miss Tisdale and Baby Faith are being kept."

"That's why I suggested we search the river for that speedboat," said Louise, but she would divulge no more of her ideas.

When they reached the settlement on the banks of the stream, they locked the car and made their way to the boathouse near the bridge, where they found Lem Wilkes, the boatman. He was very much surprised to see them.

"We thought we'd take a little pleasure cruise," smiled Uncle Ned. "That is, if your launch is still available."

Mr. Wilkes wagged his head in amazement, as if he thought a man of Uncle Ned's years should know better than to go out in an open boat in late November.

"You must be crazy, that's all I can say," he muttered. "Anybody who thinks it's fun to go out on the river at this time of year ain't quite bright."

"It takes all kinds of people to make a world," laughed Uncle Ned. "If you'll let us hire the launch——"

"Oh, sure, I'll let you have it. Glad to make a little extra money. But I still think it's a goofy way to spend the rest of the afternoon. It's mighty cold out there."

"We're well wrapped up," Jean assured him, pulling up the collar of her coat as if to prove her statement.

"By the way," asked Uncle Ned, "have there been many boats on the river lately?"

"Not pleasure boats," said Wilkes. "Well —there was one. A speedboat. It used to go up and down the river quite a bit but I haven't seen it for the past few days."

"Speedboat, eh? Which way was it heading when you last saw it?"

"South. It never came back, so I guess it's been put away for the winter."

Jean had an inspiration.

"Does this river connect with the one that runs through Oak Falls?" she asked.

"Yep," said Wilkes. "The two rivers meet about fifteen miles south of here. Say—you're not thinking of going all the way to Oak Falls tonight, are you?"

"I hardly think so," said Uncle Ned. "We may be away until dark, however. It all depends."

Mr. Wilkes's expression indicated that he

would be surprised at nothing. People who went for pleasure cruises on the river in November were nothing short of weak-minded in his opinion.

When they were out in mid-stream and heading toward the south, Captain Dana praised Jean for her question to the boatman.

"That was clever figuring on your part," he beamed, "asking about the rivers connecting."

"What was your train of thought?" asked Louise.

"Well, the letter addressed to Jacob Jacobs was to be sent to Oak Falls," she answered. "If Tepper was in Oak Falls to get the letter, he must have arrived there very soon after Miss Tisdale was taken from the house in the clearing. It seems to me that he must have gone by boat."

"Then," said Uncle Ned, "Miss Tisdale may be in Oak Falls right now. She was taken there in the speedboat."

"But how about the car Mr. Tepper was driving when the boy delivered him the bogus letter?" asked Louise.

"The woman brought that car up here to Hilton and took Baby Faith back to Oak Falls with her," replied Jean.

"There may be something in that theory," Uncle Ned agreed. "Well, it's harder to hide a boat than it is a car. I've asked the police in Oak Falls to be on the lookout for Tepper's car, and now I'm on the lookout for his boat. If we can find one or the other, we'll be a lot farther ahead."

They went down the river for about five miles until they came to a small village. Arriving there, Uncle Ned steered the launch toward a small boathouse where a man was repairing a skiff. He eyed the trio curiously as they approached.

"You must like boating," he said, "to be out on the river at this time of year."

"It isn't all pleasure," said Uncle Ned. "We are trying to get some information about a speedboat that has been traveling up and down the river the past few weeks."

"I think I know the boat you mean. It's the only pleasure craft that's been passing regularly of late. I haven't seen it for a day or so, though. The man came in here to buy some gasoline."

"What did he look like?" asked Louise quickly.

"Stout, thick-set fellow," replied the man. "He wasn't any stranger to the water, I could tell that. I'd take him for a sailor. He handled that speedboat as if he knew his business."

"A sailor, eh?" said Uncle Ned. "I don't suppose he told you his name?"

"No, he didn't. And he didn't have anything to say about his business, either, although I was a bit curious as to why he was traveling up and down the river so often.'' He winked slyly. ''Of course, there's them that don't want to talk about their business.''

Uncle Ned agreed with him.

''You haven't seen that boat on the river for several days, then?''

''No. Of course, it may have gone by at night and I mightn't have noticed it.''

By this time they were convinced that the speedboat had indeed been piloted by Sailor Tepper. The description given by the man at the boathouse seemed to settle that fact. As they resumed their journey down the stream, the Dana girls and their uncle began to reason matters out.

''If he took Miss Tisdale to Oak Falls by boat,'' said Louise, ''I think that she is probably hidden in a place very close to the river, for he would be taking a great risk bringing her into the town.''

''Yes,'' agreed Jean, ''for she would be able to call for help. And if he didn't bring her to Oak Falls, he must have stopped at some place along the river.''

''We'll go on a few miles farther and keep our eyes open for any likely places,'' added Uncle Ned.

The river wound through farming country and bushlands for several miles. At last they came within sight of a rambling building at the end of a road that sloped down toward the water. It was evidently an amusement resort of some kind, for the place was encircled by a wide veranda, and a huge sign painted on the roof read as follows:

ROSEDALE PAVILION—DANCE—EAT

"I don't feel much like dancing right now," laughed Jean, "unless it would be to keep myself warm. But I do feel like eating. I'm starved."

"So am I," said Louise. "Let's stop here and get a meal, Uncle Ned."

"It's just a summer dance pavilion," said Captain Dana. "It's probably closed up. I don't like the looks of the place, anyway. I'd rather take you to a nicer-looking place."

"It isn't closed," said Louise. "I just saw someone go in a side door."

"And I see something else," cried Jean quickly. "We *must* stop here, Uncle Ned."

She pointed toward a little wharf jutting out into the river. Tied to the dock was a craft which Jean's quick eyes had noticed when the others had overlooked it entirely.

"Tepper's speedboat!" she cried, a thrill of triumph in her voice.

CHAPTER XXI

Outwitted

THE Dana girls were tense with excitement as their launch moved toward the shore and nosed its way to the wharf. As they drew closer to the speedboat, they saw that it was indeed the craft that had almost collided with them.

"You have sharp eyes, Jean," complimented Uncle Ned softly. "I'm not doubting but that we have found the spot where Tepper is keeping Miss Tisdale—and perhaps Baby Faith as well. It's ideal for the purpose. Few people come here at this time of year. And who would suspect a dance pavilion as a hiding place?"

"There are windows upstairs," whispered Louise.

"Rooms above the restaurant part. We'll have to be careful. Perhaps he has seen us coming."

"One of us should stay and keep an eye on the speedboat," Jean suggested.

"I'll do that," volunteered Uncle Ned.

He shut off the engine and the launch drifted

slowly toward the wharf. When the boat came abreast of a slip, Uncle Ned steadied it and the two girls jumped out.

"I'll stay here," he said, tying up the craft. "No one can see me from the pavilion. The two of you go up and get the lay of the land. If Tepper is there he may recognize you, and if he does he'll probably try to run away. But he'll never reach his speedboat. I'll attend to that!"

"Suppose we don't see Tepper at all?" asked Louise, as the sisters hurried toward the amusement building.

"There'll be somebody in charge," replied Jean. "We'll ask about the speedboat, find out who owns it, and how it got here."

The Rosedale Pavilion was a shabby, desolate building, obviously used only as a river resort in the summer season, and the girls wondered that it had not been closed up weeks before.

"Tepper or no Tepper," said Jean, shivering, "I hope we can get a meal. I'm cold and hungry."

"There is smoke coming from the chimney," Louise pointed out. "That means there is probably a fire in the kitchen stove."

They went up onto the veranda and walked toward the main entrance. As they drew near an open window fronting on the porch they heard voices.

Two men were sitting at a table in a small room beyond the window. They were so engrossed in conversation that they did not hear the girls approach. In one quick instant Jean and Louise had a glimpse of the pair.

One of the men was Sailor Tepper!

Jean recognized him instantly as the man she had seen in the car in front of Lone Tree Cottage. He was leaning forward, talking earnestly to a burly, bullet-headed man in a white apron—obviously the proprietor of the place.

The girls passed the window quickly, but that one fleeting glance was enough. They were on the right trail. They had run Sailor Tepper to earth at last!

They went into the restaurant, which was not a large place, the greater part of the pavilion's space being given over to the veranda, which was used for dancing. There was a small counter, a showcase containing candy and tobacco, and about a dozen round tables.

"We'll try to get upstairs," whispered Louise excitedly as they went inside. "Miss Tisdale may be in one of the rooms up there."

A door opened and the proprietor came out. He seemed surprised to find customers in his place at that time of day.

"Good afternoon," he said agreeably. "I hope you haven't been waiting long. I didn't hear you come in. What can I do for you?"

"Could we have dinner here?" asked Louise.

"Yes, we still serve meals," he replied. "I'm closing up the place after Thanksgiving. Very few people come now that summer is over. I'm afraid we haven't much variety, but I'll ask the cook to fix up something."

"That will be very nice," said Jean. "Is there some place where we can wash our hands and fix our hair?"

"Why, you can go upstairs," he said, after a moment's hesitation. "Some of the rooms are open. You'll find mirrors and washbowls."

Elated, the Dana girls walked quickly toward the stairway and dashed up the short flight. In a few moments they were standing in a long hallway in the upper part of the building.

"If she is here at all," whispered Jean, "she is surely hidden in one of these rooms. We'll try them all."

The first door was closed. They knocked gently. No one answered, so they went on down the hall, rapping at each door in turn. Some of them were open, the rooms empty. Though they traversed the entire length of the hall and tried every door they were finally forced to the conclusion that the upper part of the building was deserted. It was a crushing disappointment.

"We've drawn a blank again," said Louise disconsolately. "She isn't here."

"I was sure we would find her hidden in one

of these rooms. No, she isn't here. But Tepper is!'' declared Jean.

"Shall we ask him?''

"Of course. We'll accuse him. He can't get away. Uncle Ned is guarding the wharf. We'll ask him where he is hiding Miss Tisdale and Baby Faith. We'll let him know that we realize he is responsible. If he refuses to talk, then we'll call in the police.''

"Let us go down and talk to him at once,'' said Louise with determination.

The girls hurried downstairs. The proprietor of the place was just coming out of the kitchen. When they saw him, Jean said:

"Is Mr. Tepper here?''

The man looked puzzled.

"Tepper?'' he said. "There's no one by that name around the place.''

"But you were talking to him not ten minutes ago,'' Louise insisted. "He was with you in that little room.''

"Oh—*that* chap! His name isn't Tepper. He's an old shipmate of mine——''

At that moment a door opened, and out into the main room stepped a short, thick-set man—Tepper himself!

A startled look flashed into his eyes when he saw the girls. He appeared confused, hesitated an instant, then stepped back as if he intended to return to the room he had just left. But Jean stepped forward quickly.

"We'd like a word with you, Mr. Tepper," she said.

He gave her a surly glance.

"My name's not Tepper, Miss," he growled.

"It may not be your real name, but it's the name we know you by," continued Jean. "We have seen you before, as you probably remember. We saw you outside Mrs. Brixton's cottage at Hilton a few days ago."

"I was never near the place in my life."

"Where are you hiding Miss Tisdale and Baby Faith?" demanded Jean firmly.

Tepper was silent for a moment. Then, with a gesture of impatience, he said:

"I don't know what you're talking about."

Before the girls could stop him he sprang toward a coat and cap that were hanging on the wall beside the door. With one quick movement he swept them from the hook and flung open the door.

"Stop him!" cried Louise.

But Tepper was already out on the wide veranda. The girls reached the door just in time to see him vault over the rail.

"Look here!" yelled the bewildered proprietor behind them. "What's the idea?"

The Danas did not wait to explain. Tepper was already running across the courtyard. The girls sped after him.

"Uncle Ned will get him," cried Jean, "when he makes for the boat."

Tepper, however, did not head for the wharf. To their surprise and alarm he ran around toward the back of the building, and when they caught sight of him again he was scrambling into an automobile which they had not noticed before.

Up to this time the girls had not raised an outcry, for they were confident that Tepper would run toward the dock, there to be easily captured by Captain Dana. But this unexpected move changed the whole situation.

"Uncle Ned! Uncle Ned!" they cried.

Tepper was already backing the car out of the courtyard. In the next instant Jean had reached it and jumped onto the running board. Then the auto shot forward, nearly flinging the girl off.

"Don't let him get away!" cried Louise.

As the car gathered speed, Tepper reached out a hairy hand, and with an iron grip threw Jean from the side of the machine. With a thud she landed in the sod.

The car skidded wildly as it reached the road, straightened out as it took the turn, and then went roaring off up the slope.

"Oh, Jean!" cried Louise, rushing to her sister. "Are you hurt?"

"Only my feelings," Jean replied, picking herself up.

Uncle Ned, running up, was all concern, but as soon as he was sure his niece was not injured beyond a couple of bruises, he became wrathful over the situation.

"After that man!" he bellowed. Then, turning to the proprietor, he shouted: "Haven't you another car?"

The man shook his head.

"That's *his* car. It's the only automobile that's been around here for days."

A cloud of dust on the hillside road testified to the haste of Tepper's departure. His flight was clearly an admission of guilt, but there was small consolation in that.

"Why didn't we think of a car?" asked Louise remorsefully. "We'll never catch him now, I'm afraid."

"Yes, we will!" declared Jean. "I'm more eager to capture him than ever. And I will!"

CHAPTER XXII

LATE AGAIN

UNCLE NED turned to the proprietor.

"What's your name?" he snapped.

"O'Grady."

"Well, then, O'Grady—if you have a telephone here, I'd advise you to get busy and notify the police in the nearest town to watch for that car and arrest that man on sight."

"It was the car the woman was driving," cried Jean. "The car Tepper drove when we saw him in Hilton. I have the number here."

She produced the slip of paper on which she had written the number. Uncle Ned gave it to O'Grady.

"There's the car number," he said. "Now get busy. And then we'll have a little talk with you. I want to know just how much you know about this affair."

"I don't know anything about any affair," said O'Grady. "If he has done anything wrong, it's the first I've heard of it."

"Get busy and telephone the police. What's the name of the nearest town?"

"Clinton. That's the exchange."

"All right. Give that car number to the Clinton police and tell them to arrest Tepper on sight."

The restaurant owner, cowed by Uncle Ned's abrupt manner, hurried back into the restaurant. Captain Dana and the girls followed, and heard him give the car number to the Clinton police, obeying the instructions to the letter.

"The two men can't be in league with each other," said Louise quietly, "or he would have tried to put the police on the wrong trail."

"Perhaps he will tell us something about Tepper," added Jean.

When O'Grady finished his conversation, he came over to them. His face wore a worried look.

"I wish you'd tell me what the trouble is," he said. "I don't know very much about that man, but if he's been up to mischief, I haven't had anything to do with it. He's an old shipmate of mine."

"Shipmate, eh?" said Uncle Ned. "You've been a sailor?"

"Aye, sir. I gave up sailing about five years ago."

"My name is Dana."

"Not Captain Dana of the *Balaska!*" exclaimed O'Grady. He saluted. "I've often heard of you, Captain." His manner, which had been hostile, altered at once. "If there's anything I can do for you, Captain, I'm at your service. As for this man you call Tepper—I never knew him by that name. He was a ship-mate of mine on a tramp steamer out of New Orleans several years ago, but I always knew him as 'Red Pepper.' That's the name he went by then.''

" 'Red Pepper'!" exclaimed Captain Dana. "Ah! I know the fellow. He once sailed with me. He's a crook if there ever was one."

"Well, I don't know about that, sir. I only knew him on the one voyage. He showed up here a few weeks ago and we recognized each other. He has been in here a few times."

"Is that his speedboat down by the wharf?"

"No," said O'Grady, "it's mine."

"Yours? But Tepper was running it!"

"I lent it to him a few times. He said he wanted to take a few trips up the river."

"Well, O'Grady," said Uncle Ned, "I think you're an honest man. I don't believe you knew what Tepper was up to, but I'm warning you now that you had better collar him and lock him up and call the police if he shows his nose around here again. He's a bad customer, and you might have got yourself into serious trouble by being friendly with him."

O'Grady, frightened and impressed, anxiously insisted that he knew nothing of any wrong-doing. Questioned further by Uncle Ned, he could throw no light on Tepper's movements beyond the fact that the sailor had made a number of trips up the river in the speedboat.

"Did he always land here?"

"He always brought the boat back to this wharf."

"Did he bring anyone with him?"

"None that I ever saw. He brought the boat back here one night—after I had closed up and gone to bed. I found it at the wharf next morning. He might have taken someone with him that time."

"Where does he live?"

"He said he lived in Oak Falls. He always came out here in his car."

"What reason did he give for these trips up the river?" asked Jean.

"Well, being a sailor, he had a fondness for the water. He said he was thinking of buying a little farm along the water and settling down. He wanted to look over some of the properties around here."

Uncle Ned sighed heavily.

"I'm afraid Sailor Tepper won't come around any more. The search will have to center in Oak Falls now. Well, I suppose we may as well stay here and have supper. Then we'll go back upstream in the launch."

Louise looked at her watch.

"Half-past six!" she exclaimed. "We'll be late again. What will Mrs. Crandall say?"

"She shouldn't scold you," said Uncle Ned

comfortingly. "After all, it was done for a good cause."

Supper was soon ready, and they all enjoyed a hearty meal before setting out on their return journey. O'Grady, frightened by the knowledge that he had been helping and sheltering a crook, was eager to create a good impression and did his best to make them feel comfortable and at home. They were satisfied by now that he had been an innocent victim of circumstances. When they finally said goodbye to him on the wharf, he promised to do all he could to help them.

"I'm afraid Tepper won't show up again," said O'Grady, "but if he does, I'll be ready for him. He won't make a fool of me a second time!"

It was very dark when they started their homeward journey. The girls were dismally convinced that a scolding awaited them on their return to Starhurst, and this prospect did not brighten the cold journey on the black river. In the teeth of a biting breeze, the launch forged steadily upstream.

It was after nine o'clock when they finally reached Starhurst. As they had feared, Mrs. Crandall was waiting up for them. She met them in the hall. Her greeting was severe.

"It appears to me," she said frigidly, "that the rules of the school mean little or nothing to you two girls."

"We are very sorry, Mrs. Crandall," said Louise apologetically. "We didn't intend to stay out so late."

"I am not inclined to overlook this," said Mrs. Crandall, in icy tones. "You cannot expect to receive favors which are not granted to the other girls. I have already received several complaints. You are upsetting the morale of the school."

"If you'll just let me explain, Mrs. Crandall," said Uncle Ned, "I'll tell you how it happened. It's all my fault——"

"No explanations are necessary, Captain Dana. I have been very generous, I think, in overlooking your nieces' continual absences. It seems that their outside visiting occupies more of their time than their school work. I can't permit it. When other students complain, I must take action. This nonsense must cease immediately. Jean and Louise, unless you are prepared to live up to the rules of Starhurst, I shall have to ask you to leave the school."

"We don't want to leave Starhurst, Mrs. Crandall," said Louise.

"You won't have any further cause for complaint, Mrs. Crandall," said Captain Dana. "Run along upstairs and get some sleep, girls, and I'll have a little chat with your principal. Maybe I'll be able to persuade her that I'm the one she ought to be scolding."

The sisters hurried to their study.

"After all," admitted Jean, "we have been spending a great deal of time on the mystery. We can scarcely blame Mrs. Crandall."

"Not if she has been receiving complaints. But who would have done such a thing? She said the complaints had come from other students."

"I can guess."

"So can I."

"Lettie Briggs is at the bottom of this," said Jean.

"And her shadow, Ina Mason."

CHAPTER XXIII

The Hounds

Captain Dana, who had spent the night at the Tisdales', came to Starhurst early next morning and saw his nieces for a few minutes before classes.

"I can't stay long," he said, "but I just wanted to tell you not to worry too much about what Mrs. Crandall said last night. It seems that a couple of the other girls were making a fuss about your being out so much. However, I fixed everything up. I explained that you were doing the best you could to find Miss Tisdale and Baby Faith. She said it was a matter for the police, but I persuaded her differently."

"I suppose we hardly dare ask for a holiday today," ventured Jean.

"You get no holiday today!" declared Uncle Ned emphatically. "That goes for me, as well as for Mrs. Crandall."

"But can't we take this afternoon off?"

"After classes you may. I'll call for you. In the meantime, I'm going to Lone Tree Cottage to find out if there have been any new developments. Chances are we'll have Tepper in jail and Miss Tisdale and the baby back home safe and sound before school's out.''

"That would be just our luck," declared Louise, her eyes showing her disappointment. "After all the work we've done on the mystery, too.''

"Perhaps the police at Clinton have found Tepper already," said Jean.

Captain Dana shook his head.

"I telephoned to Clinton last night and again this morning. They're still looking for that car. They haven't found any trace of it. I'm thinking that this fellow Tepper, or Pepper, or whatever his name is—well, I'm thinking he is a mighty slippery customer.''

Although the girls wanted to talk longer to their guardian, this was not possible as the bell for classes was ringing.

"Oh, dear!" exclaimed Jean, as they hastened toward their classrooms. "I can't bear the thought of that English examination today.''

"I'm not enjoying the prospect of mine, either," Louise admitted. "But we shan't dare get low marks.''

They realized that they had been doing their extra reading in hit-or-miss fashion, almost all their spare time being occupied with the mystery, and they were not looking forward to their examinations with a feeling of confidence.

Jean's worst fears were realized when she read the English paper assigned to her class by Miss Cleek. It was, as Jean put it, "a terror." It was the stiffest examination paper in English that had ever been placed before the students. Miss Cleek sat at her desk and eyed the class grimly, as if to say: "Now, we'll see if that other English teacher taught you anything."

Ruefully Jean attacked the questions and did the best she could with them. But she was conscious that they were too involved for her —particularly those which had to do with *David Copperfield*.

"Even Charles Dickens himself would have been stumped by several of those questions," declared Jean when the examination was over.

Some of the other girls crowded around, eager to hear how everyone felt about the ordeal. They all agreed that the paper had been unusually severe, and the fervent hope was expressed that Miss Tisdale would be back at Starhurst to resume her duties after the Thanksgiving vacation.

When classes were dismissed for the day, the girls sighed with relief and anticipation. As they went up to their rooms, Louise said, "I hope Uncle Ned won't be late. We dare not miss dinner tonight."

When they opened the study door, they were relieved to find Captain Dana already waiting for them. He sat placidly in an armchair near the window, reading a newspaper.

"I thought I'd come along a few minutes early," he explained. "Not that it makes any difference. I think we shan't be able to do much work on the mystery this afternoon—and I want you to come back to Oak Falls with me tomorrow."

"Then you've made no progress at all?" asked Jean disappointedly, though trying all the while to hide her true feelings.

"Nary a bit. I've been in touch with Boltwood, the detective, with the police in Clinton, and with O'Grady out at the pavilion, but there's nothing to report. Our friend Tepper seems to have vanished into thin air."

"No ransom message?" asked Louise.

"None. I was rather expecting that the Tisdales would get a letter of some kind, but there was nothing. I think Tepper will lie low for a few days before he makes another move."

"How is Mrs. Brixton?"

"All broken up, poor creature. Mr. and Mrs. Tisdale are doing the best they can to comfort her, but only one thing matters to her now. She wants Baby Faith back."

"But can't we do *anything*?" demanded Louise.

Captain Dana shrugged his shoulders, while a look of despair came over his face.

"What can we do? You found Miss Tisdale

once, and lost her again. We found Tepper, and lost *him* again. The police are looking for the car but they can't find it. We've located the speedboat, but it doesn't belong to Tepper at all. All the clues are used up. We're facing a blank wall. We're beaten. There's only one thing to do now. Tepper will get in touch with the Tisdales sooner or later and demand the five thousand dollars. Mr. Tisdale says he is prepared to pay it."

"But will Tepper return Miss Tisdale and Baby Faith even then?" asked Louise. "He may demand more money."

"Perhaps. Mr. Tisdale will have to take a chance on that."

Jean was thoughtful, a frown puckering her otherwise smooth brow.

"You say we have used up all the clues, Uncle Ned. But I think not."

"The car, the speedboat, the house in the woods——"

"You have forgotten the hounds."

"The hounds? What about them?" asked Uncle Ned.

"Where did they go when the house was abandoned? Where did Tepper hide them? It isn't easy to hide four big dogs. I have my own ideas about the hounds. I believe they were taken away by boat. And I'm going to call up Mr. O'Grady, at the Rosedale Pavilion, and ask him about them."

Uncle Ned was dubious. Nevertheless, he agreed that there was a chance—a slim chance —that O'Grady might know something about the dogs. They went downstairs and asked permission to use the telephone. Louise looked up the Rosedale Pavilion in the directory and gave Jean the number.

They waited, expectantly, when Jean gave the operator the number. Finally came the word:

"I'm sorry. There is no answer."

"Please try again," urged Jean. She felt that it was their last opportunity to solve the mystery. Should they be obliged to return to Oak Falls with Uncle Ned the following day the case would be at an end, so far as they were concerned.

"I'm sorry," said the operator finally. "The number does not——"

She was interrupted by a deep voice which boomed: "Hello! Hello! Someone calling the Rosedale Pavilion?"

Jean's heart jumped. It was the voice of O'Grady, the proprietor.

"Here is your party," said the operator.

"Hello! Mr. O'Grady?" asked Jean, and received an affirmative reply. "This is Jean Dana. My sister and I were at your place yesterday afternoon with Captain Dana."

"Yes. I remember," said O'Grady. "I'm mighty sorry, Miss, but I haven't any news for you. That fellow didn't show up. I guess he's scared to come around here again."

"Your boat is still there?"

"Yes, Miss. It is. I have it locked up, too, in case he might be tempted to come around and borrow it while I'm not looking."

"I'm going to ask you an odd question, Mr. O'Grady," continued Jean.

"Go ahead. I'm glad to do anything I can to help you."

"Do you know if Mr. Tepper owned any dogs?"

"Dogs? I should say so. He owned four of the wickedest hounds I ever saw in my life."

"Hounds! You say you *saw* them?"

"Indeed, and I did. He had them at my place for a day or so. Brought them down the river in the boat one time. Seemed in an awful hurry. He asked me to look after them. I meant to tell you about them yesterday, but it slipped my mind."

"Then the hounds are not there now?"

"No," said O'Grady. "Red Pepper came and took them away again."

"When?"

"Yesterday morning. I was glad to see them go, too, I can tell you. They were fierce brutes."

"Where did he go with them?"

"Why, he took them away in the boat."

"In the boat!" exclaimed Jean, now wildly

excited. "But the boat was tied up to your wharf."

"He took the boat up the river in the morning," explained O'Grady, "and the dogs went with him. He came back without the dogs, tied the boat to the wharf, and then came up into the pavilion to talk to me."

"Thank you, Mr. O'Grady," said Jean. "Thank you *very, very* much."

"Don't mention it, Miss. I should have told you about the dogs yesterday, I guess, but I——"

Jean replaced the receiver, and hurriedly turned to Louise and Uncle Ned.

"There's our clue!" she cried excitedly. "Now I think I know where we can find Miss Tisdale and Baby Faith!"

CHAPTER XXIV

The Old Woman

"What's this?" said Uncle Ned. "You think you know? What did O'Grady tell you? Why were you asking him about the hounds?"

Quickly Jean explained what she had learned from O'Grady.

"The dogs were taken down the river to the pavilion when Tepper was frightened away. Yesterday he took the dogs back up the river again. He must have taken them *back* to the house in the woods. And that's where Miss Tisdale and Baby Faith are hidden now."

"Jean! You've hit it!" cried Louise joyously. "Why didn't we think of that before? Tepper figured it would never occur to us to search the house in the clearing again so he simply went right back to it."

"I believe there's something to that idea," agreed Uncle Ned. "I'm all for getting a few policemen and going out there right away. Jean, you've a good head on your shoulders."

More hopeful of success than they had been at any time since the mystery began, they hastily left the school and drove to the Penfield

203

police station. The sergeant in charge recognized the girls at once.

"So!" he said. "The young ladies who brought us on that wild-goose chase into the woods a few nights ago. Well, what is it this time?"

"We want you to send some men out there with us again," said Louise.

The sergeant frowned.

"Nothing doing," he said.

Captain Dana intervened.

"But this is serious, Sergeant," he said.

"It was serious last time, too. And all we found was an empty house."

"But we believe the people came back to it. The dogs were taken down the river, and we have just received information to the effect that they were brought back up the river again by boat. This is a serious matter, Sergeant. A woman and a child have been spirited away and they may be hidden in that house."

The sergeant was curious.

"It's the first we've heard of it," he said. "We have no record of any disappearance like that."

"The police weren't informed," interposed Captain Dana. "It's a question of ransom."

Quickly Uncle Ned explained the details of the case. The time for concealment, he felt, was past. And, as he told the story, the sergeant's skepticism vanished.

"I'll go out there with you myself," he said. "We'll bring along six men, and we'll post some of them at the river and some in the woods. If those people are at the house now, they won't slip through our fingers this time."

There was hasty activity in the police station. Curtly the sergeant gave instructions to his men. Jean and Louise were very tense, their nerves keyed to the highest pitch.

"If we have guessed wrong," said Jean, "I'll never be able to look a policeman in the eye again."

"They'll be wild!" admitted Louise. "But I'm sure we're right, Jean. We *can't* be wrong this time."

Nevertheless, the girls were apprehensive as they drove away from the police station a few minutes later, followed by a department automobile containing the sergeant and his half dozen burly constables. They dreaded the ridicule and the justifiable anger of the policemen should the house in the woods again prove to be deserted.

"We'll have to take the chance," said Uncle Ned. "If we were to go out there first to spy out the ground, we should probably be seen."

When the police car reached the side road that led from the main highway toward the woods, it came to a stop. Two constables got out and were instructed to go down to the river and work their way along the bank so as to cut off any escape that might be attempted by water. Later, when the party reached the woods at the end of the road, two other constables were detailed to circle around through the bush to cover both sides of the clearing. Every possible way of escape was thus cut off.

"Now," said the sergeant gruffly, "we'll raid that house again. And this time there had better be someone at home!"

He cast the girls a meaning glance as he spoke. Meekly they followed at his heels as he went down the path in the direction of the clearing.

"I do hope we haven't guessed wrong!" whispered Jean.

At that very moment a deep, mournful sound rang out on the autumn air. It was the baying of a hound! It was followed a few seconds later by a doleful howl. Then the woods echoed with the resonant clamor of the dogs.

"You were right, Jean!" cried Louise. "The dogs *were* brought back."

The sergeant broke into a run. Captain Dana was close at his side. The uproar of the dogs could mean but one thing—the house in the woods was no longer deserted. The girls were almost beside themselves with excitement, for they felt that the end of the long pursuit of Tepper was at hand. By the time they came in sight of the clearing, the hounds were creating an indescribable clamor. The huge dogs could be seen leaping and plunging toward the wire fence.

The policemen had come prepared for the hounds, having armed themselves with four large nets, borrowed for the occasion from the Penfield dog-catcher. Uncle Ned and the sergeant were in the lead, and advanced toward the fence.

"Must be a gate around here somewhere!" said Captain Dana. "Ah! There it is. Over to the left. Come on, Sergeant!"

Jean and Louise came with them as far as the high gate. They watched the house carefully but could see no sign of life save the huge hounds. They looked for the window at which they had seen Miss Tisdale, but it was closed.

"Regular fortress, this place," declared the sergeant when they reached the gate. He indicated a large padlock which held the portal securely locked. The animals, barking furiously, came rushing toward them, hurling themselves wildly against the netting. The sergeant took a whistle from his pocket and blew a shrill blast.

"We'll see if there's anyone at home," he said.

Scarcely had the sounds died away than they saw a movement at one of the windows in the upper part of the house. The window was slowly thrust open.

An old woman, white-haired and wearing

spectacles, leaned out over the sill. Angrily she called to the dogs:

"You, Rover! You, Pete! Go and lie down. Stop that barking. Go and lie down, I say!"

Her voice was cracked and high-pitched, but it had a magical effect on the dogs. They ceased their howling instantly and slunk back toward the house where they huddled in a group near the shed, still watching the people at the gate.

"Now, then," called out the old woman harshly, "what do you want? Why do you come here disturbing honest people?"

"We're looking for a man named Tepper!" called out Uncle Ned.

"Tepper? You've made a mistake," insisted the cackling old woman. "No one by that name lives here. This house belongs to the Laytons. They're all away for the winter. I'm here alone. You've got the wrong house. Go away."

The sergeant bit his lip in exasperation.

"She's right, at that," he said. "After we came back from here the other day, I looked up this house. It does belong to a family named Layton."

"Who owns the dogs?" demanded Uncle Ned.

"I own the dogs!" declared the old woman. "I keep them here for my own protection. Now go away from here and leave me alone. I don't want to be disturbed. I don't know anything about this Mr. Tepper you're talking about. He doesn't live here."

"Another false alarm," growled the sergeant in disgust. "There's nothing doing here."

"But the dogs belong to Tepper!" cried Louise. "He must have been here. I believe that isn't an old woman at all. I think it's Tepper or an accomplice in disguise. We must get into the house."

The sergeant rubbed his chin dubiously.

"Disguise, eh?" he said. "I didn't think of that. You may be right."

He called out to the figure at the window.

"We're coming in. Open the gate."

"You're not coming in here!" shrilled the old woman. "I'll set the dogs on you You've got the wrong house, I tell you. Go away."

She uttered a sharp command to the hounds. Instantly they came racing across the yard, fangs bared, their eyes red with fury. It seemed that the animals were bent on leaping over the gate. The sergeant suddenly pulled a revolver from his holster and fired into the air.

The sound of the shot had a remarkable effect upon the dogs. They yelped in fear. They fell back, whining. The sergeant seized a net from one of his constables and scrambled up over the gate. The two other policemen followed. Uncle Ned also seized a net and clambered over the barrier.

The cowed brutes offered little resistance. Within a few minutes they were yelping and whining in fear as they struggled vainly in the meshes of the nets, now quite helpless to do any damage. While all this was going on the old woman in the window shrieked commands that the intruders leave the premises at once. Finally, seeing that they had no intention of doing so, she closed the window with a bang and vanished.

"Come on, Jean," cried Louise, seeing that there was no further danger from the hounds. "I'm sure Tepper is in that house."

They ran hastily up the rough path that led to the front door. As they approached the house, they heard a woman's scream.

"Help! Help!"

CHAPTER XXV

The Dana Girls' Triumph

'It's Miss Tisdale!'' cried Jean.

The girls rushed toward the house. The police sergeant, however, reached the door first. He flung himself against it, but it resisted all his efforts to force it open.

"Watch the back entrance!" shouted the sergeant to one of his men. "Come on, Captain Dana! Lend a hand here."

Uncle Ned did not lend a hand. He lent a shoulder, and as he and the sergeant hurled themselves against the wooden panels, the lock gave with a sharp snap, and the door fell open. The two men tumbled into the hall beyond.

They were just in time to spy someone running down the corridor. It was the old woman they had seen at the window. The sergeant overtook her at a bound and seized her by the arm. She turned around, screaming and struggling. Her spectacles became disarranged, her white hair was awry.

"Just as Louise suspected!" said Uncle Ned.

He snatched at the woman's head, and the mass of white hair came away in his hands.

It was a wig. The spectacles fell off. Instead of a feeble old woman, the prisoner was revealed to his surprise as a frightened woman of middle age.

"Don't touch me!" she cried.

"Where's Tepper?" demanded Captain Dana.

"I don't know what you mean. I never heard of him."

At that moment there was a shout from the rear of the building. It was followed by a bellow of rage, then by sounds of a struggle. The back door crashed open. Into the house came two policemen, clinging firmly to a man who kicked and struggled vainly to free himself.

The man was Sailor Tepper!

When the woman saw him, she became quieter.

"I guess it's all up, Sol," she muttered sullenly. "They've got us."

"We'd never have been caught if it hadn't been for those confounded girls," snarled Tepper.

"Caught him trying to make a get-away out the back door," said one of the policemen. He wrenched a pair of handcuffs from his pocket, and snapped them about Tepper's wrists.

"Where is Miss Tisdale?" cried Louise.

"And the baby," added Jean.

Tepper glared at them menacingly.

"Not in this place!" he shouted. "They're where you'll never find them."

The girls had not forgotten the screams they had heard as they approached the house. Louise whirled around and ran up the stairs, with Jean close at her heels. Swiftly they searched the upper rooms of the house. But they were empty.

"There's a stairway to the attic!" cried Jean. As they ran up the steps they could hear sounds of sobbing from beyond a door at the top of the flight. It was the voice of a child, crying. Louise tried the door but it was locked.

"Miss Tisdale!" she cried, pounding at the door. "Are you there?"

"Oh, thank goodness, someone has come!"

It was the voice of the missing teacher.

Louise rattled the knob frantically. Then, suddenly, she discovered that the key was in the lock. She turned it, the door fell open, and in another moment Miss Tisdale, weeping with joy, was in their arms. Baby Faith, sobbing with terror, was crouching on a low cot near the window. Jean rushed over to her and hugged the child.

Heavy footsteps pounded on the stairs. One of the policemen appeared in the doorway. He surveyed the scene and grinned.

"Everything is O.K.!" he shouted back down to those below. "They're found."

Neither Miss Tisdale nor Faith showed any ill effects from their imprisonment. The teacher alternately laughed and cried, so great was her relief.

"Oh, I thought you would never, never think of coming back here," she told the girls. "I would have tried to escape if it hadn't been for little Faith. I couldn't leave her alone, and yet I knew I should have very little chance of escaping if I tried to take her with me."

There was so much to explain that Miss Tisdale did not attempt to tell the entire story of her unpleasant experience just then. It was not until later, when Uncle Ned and the Dana girls brought her safely back to Lone Tree Cottage with Baby Faith, that all the odd angles of the affair were cleared up.

Despair and sadness gave way to tumultuous joy. Lone Tree Cottage was a scene of wild happiness. Mr. and Mrs. Tisdale were in the seventh heaven of delight when they realized that their daughter and grandchild had been restored. As for Alice Brixton, the poor widow could only cling silently to Baby Faith, kissing the child's rosy cheeks and golden hair, her eyes eloquent with relief and gratitude. Jean and Louise knew then the deep happiness that comes from sharing that of others.

"Why, I feel ten years younger!" cried old Mr. Tisdale delightedly, his eyes sparkling, as he picked Baby Faith up in his arms and proceeded to become acquainted with the grand-child whom he had never seen until this moment. "I do declare I feel better already."

"And you look it!" said his wife. "If your heart can stand all this, it can stand anything."

Old Mr. Tisdale appeared to have forgotten that he was an invalid. The cares of years seemed to have been cast aside with his recon-ciliation with his daughter and the recovery of the missing relatives.

"I never did think you were as ill as you made out to be," grinned Uncle Ned.

Miss Tisdale's story was soon told. When she had been lured from the school by the bogus note, she had driven straight toward Hilton, in the belief that Baby Faith had disappeared. Her car had been forced off the road by Sailor Tepper, who had compelled her to enter his own car, exactly as the Dana girls had deduced. She had been taken to the house in the woods, which Tepper and his wife had coolly occupied when they learned that the owners were to be away for the winter.

There she had been held prisoner, and was forced to write the notes demanding ransom. By means of the code, however, she had always contradicted the original messages without Tepper's knowledge, for she hoped that she would eventually escape or else be found. The Teppers had taken her to Oak Falls in the speedboat when the Dana girls first located the house in the clearing, but they had brought her back again as soon as they believed the danger had blown over. Suspecting that something was wrong, Tepper had determined to make sure of the ransom by stealing Baby Faith, and his wife had been sent to Hilton on this errand. Both had been well treated, but it had been Tepper's full intention to keep them as prisoners until the entire amount of the ransom should be forthcoming.

"Thanks to these clever girls, however," said Mrs. Tisdale, "the whole plot has been broken up. My dears, we can never, never tell you how grateful we are to you for what you have done for us."

"It was fun!" said Jean.

"You must drop in to see us whenever you can," urged Mr. Tisdale, shaking their hands warmly. "Alice and the baby will come to live with us, of course. Lone Tree Cottage is —er—too lonesome—and I think they'll be more comfortable—with us. I've been a stubborn, foolish old man, but I want to make amends for it while I can."

Alice Brixton kissed him happily. "Of course we'll come to live with you, Father. And now, Amy won't have to teach school any more to support me."

Miss Tisdale laughed.

"Oh, but I love teaching. I wouldn't give it up for the world." Then she looked anxiously at the girls. "I do hope they haven't given my position to someone else."

"They did," said Louise, "but I'm sure you'll have no trouble in getting it back. Why, Starhurst wouldn't be the same without you, Miss Tisdale."

Any anxieties the instructor might have had on that score were set at rest by Mrs. Crandall, when the girls returned to Starhurst that night. They were late again—but what of that? Uncle Ned gleefully explained all the circumstances to her.

"I can't scold you, of course," she said, smiling. "Besides, we are really into the Thanksgiving holidays now. Are you going to Oak Falls for the vacation?"

"Indeed they are," declared Uncle Ned. "But I doubt if it's a recess from school work. They seem to have spent most of their time solving mysteries instead."

Mrs. Crandall laughed.

"I'm afraid I have been a trifle cross at times, Captain Dana. They'll make up for any studies they have missed, I'm sure. After all, they have united a family and brought a great deal of happiness to Mr. and Mrs. Tisdale. I'm tempted to praise them very highly."

"Don't do that," begged Uncle Ned, "or they'll be getting too big for their shoes altogether. When they come back to Starhurst after the Thanksgiving vacation, see that they work hard." He burst into such a roar of laughter that Jean and Louise could scarcely determine whether they were being scolded or praised.

"Anyway, I hope we find another mystery during our vacation," teased Jean, entirely unaware that the secret "In the Shadow of the Tower" awaited her and her sister.

"Run upstairs now and pack your things, the two of you," he ordered. "We'll drive back to Oak Falls tonight, and I know your Aunt Harriet will be impatient to hear all about it."

"About what, Uncle Ned?" asked Jean innocently.

"Don't you think she's been reading your letters? Don't you suppose she knows why I came to Starhurst ahead of time? Why, she's been on pins and needles ever since the affair began. She'll want to know all about the secret at Lone Tree Cottage, and we'd better not keep her waiting much longer."